THE WORLD'S GREATEST CHOCOLATE-

COVERED PORK CHOPS

THE WORLD'S GREATEST CHOCOLATE-COVERED PORK CHOPS

Ryan K. Sager

DISNEP • HYPERION

Los Angeles   New York

For Kate,

I love you more than chocolate.

(Don't tell chocolate.)

First Edition, June 2017
10 9 8 7 6 5 4 3 2 1
FAC-020093-17125
Printed in the United States of America

This book is set in Sabon, Rockwell, Times New Roman/Fontspring
Designed by Joann Hill

Library of Congress Cataloging-in-Publication Data
Names: Sager, Ryan K., author.
Title: The world's greatest chocolate-covered pork chops / Ryan K. Sager.
Description: First Edition. Los Angeles ; New York : Disney/Hyperion, 2017.
Summary: "Follow the adventures of plucky twelve-year-old Zoey Kate as
she opens up a restaurant inside a San Francisco trolley car"—Provided
by publisher.
Identifiers: LCCN 2016022981 • ISBN 9781484767610 (hardcover)
• ISBN 1484767616 (hardcover)
Subjects: CYAC: Cooking—Fiction. Business enterprises—Fiction.
Trolley cars—Fiction. San Francisco (Calif.)—Fiction.
Classification: LCC PZ7.1.S243 Wo 2017 • DDC [Fic]—dc23
LC record available at https://lccn.loc.gov/2016022981

Reinforced binding
Visit www.DisneyBooks.com

When's lunch?
—*Confucius*

Little Chef, Big Money

"HELP!" Zoey burst into the banker's office like wildfire on a greasy hibachi grill. *"STOP EVERYTHING! THIS IS AN EMERGENCY! HEEEEEELP!"*

The banker sprang from her chair, her eyes wider than Krispy Kreme donuts. "What's wrong? Are you in danger? Are you hurt?"

"Worse!" Zoey paused to catch her breath. "There are seven billion people in this world, and only three hundred and twenty-nine of them have tasted my delicious cooking!"

The banker glowered. "That's not an emergency."

"It feels like an emergency."

"It's not."

"Well, it should be." Zoey reached across the desk, grabbed the banker's right hand, and gave it a hearty shake. "Pleased to meet you! I'm Zoey Kate, culinary prodigy, gourmet innovator, child chef extraordinaire. Let's get started, shall we? I need fifty thousand dollars by Friday. Thursday, if possible. I prefer cash, but I'm willing to do direct deposit. Do I need to sign something, or does that handshake cover us?"

Zoey plopped onto a stiff leather chair in front of the desk. She straightened her fluffy pink chef hat (a toque, it's called) and unbuttoned the collar of her pink chef jacket. She swung her legs over the armrest, smoothing her black skirt over her black-and-white-striped leggings. Balmy June sunlight shone through the office windows, making her purple Doc Martens boots sparkle like candy wrappers.

The banker (Miss Lemon was her name) retook her seat. Her eyes narrowed like strips of raw bacon on a hot griddle. "How old are you?"

Zoey smiled. Her teeth were straight and whiter than marshmallows. "In ten short months, I'll be a sage thirteen."

"Where are your parents?"

"At work."

"Do they know you're here?"

"Of course."

"And they're okay with you borrowing fifty thousand dollars?"

"Yeah." Zoey rubbed the tip of her nose with the back of her index finger. "Why wouldn't they be?"

"Fifty thousand dollars is a lot of money for someone your age."

"Don't worry. I'll pay it all back." Zoey reached into her tangerine nylon purse, pulled out a crisp two-page document, and laid it on the desk. "Here's my loan application. Fair warning, it may blow your mind."

Wary but curious, Miss Lemon put on her mint-green reading glasses and perused the application. It consisted of ten questions, typed, with space below each question for the applicant's written responses. Miss Lemon had reviewed thousands of loan applications, but she'd never seen one quite like this. Zoey's responses were written in neon pink and lime-green ink, and all the *i*'s and *j*'s were dotted with tiny drawings of croissants and cinnamon rolls.

"It says here, Zoey, that you want this money to open—"

"The greatest restaurant in San Francisco! Well, not *just* San Francisco. I'll also open greatest restaurants in LA, New York, London, Paris, Berlin, Sydney, Dubai, et cetera. I got a ten-year plan. But let's not get ahead of ourselves. Please, one city at a time."

"And what kind of food will you serve?"

Zoey made a *hmmm-how-should-I-explain-this?* face. (If you've ever asked your dad why he spends so much time in the garage whenever your mom's parents are in town, you've seen it.) She tucked an errant strand of cheesecake-colored hair up into her toque. "I do a lot of . . . *juxtaposition.*"

"Go on."

"I combine ingredients that at first glance shouldn't go together. But they do go together, they just have to be handled right. That's what I do. I handle them right, and they become delicious." Zoey slid her legs off the armrest. "What's the matter, did you run out of bergamot?"

The change of topic was so sudden it made Miss Lemon flinch. She glanced at the half-empty tea mug on her desk. "How did you . . . ?"

Zoey sniffed. "Black tea leaves, African. Milk. Cornflowers. Vanilla. Props for making it yourself. Attempting to, at least." Zoey picked up the mug, peered inside, gave the contents a gentle swirl. "I don't blame you for not drinking much. It ain't Earl Grey without bergamot."

Miss Lemon didn't know how to respond to that, so she moved on. "I'm troubled by the answers on your application. For example, where it says, 'What is your business plan?' you wrote, 'I'll cook amazing food and people will pay me loads of money to let them eat it.'"

Zoey set down the mug. "That's right."

"Under 'Professional Training,' you wrote, 'Don't need it. I'm already awesome.'"

"Yep."

"Under 'Skills and Qualifications,' you wrote, 'Think Leonardo da Vinci, but with food.'"

"It was him or Mozart. I went back and forth."

Miss Lemon's mint-green plastic fingernails drummed on the desktop, in sync with the squeaks of a rusty ceiling fan. "Zoey, have you ever worked in a restaurant?"

"I cook food in my house every day. People are crazy about it."

"I mean a real restaurant, like Bistro Central Parc or Hawker Fare."

The muscles in Zoey's jaw tensed. "Not . . . like you mean . . . no."

"That's what I thought." Miss Lemon pushed her glasses up the bridge of her nose. "Since you've never worked in a real restaurant, how could you possibly know how to *run* a real restaurant?"

Zoey shrugged. "How hard could it be?"

"There's a lot of bookkeeping."

"I'll get a bookshelf."

"It's time-consuming."

"I'll get a day planner."

"It's stressful."

"I'll get massages."

In a corner of the room, a watercooler burped.

Miss Lemon placed the application facedown on the desk. She leaned forward, clasping her hands and interlocking her fingers on the desktop. "What do you suppose my boss would say if I told him I lent fifty thousand dollars to a twelve-year-old with no real restaurant experience?"

"That you're a captain of industry and a woman of sophistication and taste?"

"He'd fire me."

Zoey gave a sly wink. "There's a job for you in my restaurant if he does."

Miss Lemon slid the loan application to the edge of her desk. "I'm sorry, but Mulberry Bank cannot invest in you at this time."

"Loud and clear." Zoey picked a speck of basil off her sleeve. "So do I get the fifty grand now, or will you mail me a check?"

"Wow." Miss Lemon removed her glasses and massaged the bridge of her nose. "I'm going to try this again, Zoey. Please, for the love of Gordon Ramsay, listen closely. Your loan application—this one, here on my desk—is declined. That means no money. You get nothing. Nada. Zilch. Think of any number, multiply it by zero, and that's how much money this bank will lend you."

Zoey gasped. "Miss Lemon, what are you saying?"

Miss Lemon rubbed her temples like she had a headache. Or the beginnings of an aneurysm. "I am saying that Mulberry Bank will not lend you fifty thousand dollars."

Zoey slid to the edge of her seat. "Miss Lemon, you look famished. What did you eat for breakfast this morning?"

Miss Lemon's empty stomach grumbled. "I don't have time for breakfast."

Zoey clapped her hands to her cheeks. "You haven't eaten all day? It's almost noon. You must be starving! I live twelve minutes from here. Come to my house. I'll make you the best lunch you've ever had. We'll finish this conversation on a full stomach."

"I'd rather not."

"You sure? I make a mean plate of Balsamic Pear Ravioli."

"I'm sure."

"I can make it lactose-free, if that's an issue."

"It's not."

"Lactose intolerance is nothing to be ashamed of."

"I'm not lactose intolerant."

"Great!" Zoey leapt to her feet. "Wait until you see what I'm making for dessert. You'll think you've died and gone to Switzerland."

Miss Lemon groaned. "I haven't agreed to come to your house—"

"Should we walk or take a taxi? We could take the bus, but I hate the bus."

"You're not listening—"

"Lots of weirdos ride the bus. They always sit next to me. Not sure why—"

"Zoey, stop!"

Zoey stopped.

Miss Lemon was on her feet, her palms planted on the desk, her limbs as stiff as uncooked asparagus. "I am not coming to your house for lunch, and I am not, under any circumstances, authorizing your loan."

"I'll give you a minute to decide."

"No, Zoey. That's my final word."

Zoey took a small black box from her purse. The box was three cubic inches in size, with sleek black sides and edges, and wrapped in a pink ribbon. Zoey placed the box on the desk.

Miss Lemon eyed the box with suspicion. "What's this?"

"A little something I cooked up. Relax. Open it."

Sitting back down, Miss Lemon unwrapped the pink ribbon and removed the lid. Inside the box sat a white chocolate truffle cradled in a pleated black cup, curls of dark chocolate frolicking on its creamy top.

"Go ahead," Zoey said. "Try it."

Miss Lemon's pupils expanded like vanilla poured into warm milk. "Well, I wouldn't want to be rude. . . ." She withdrew the truffle from the box, stripped away the black parchment, and popped the dainty treat into her mouth. Her eyes closed. "Mmmmm."

Zoey leaned forward. "What do you taste?"

"I taste . . . chocolate, of course . . . dark chocolate . . . and traces of . . ." One eyebrow raised. "Is that . . . jalapeño?"

"Delectable, isn't it?"

"Yes, but . . . dark chocolate and jalapeño . . . together . . . who would make such a thing?"

"Don't fight it," Zoey said, her voice as soft as hot

caramel. "Surrender to the flavors. Let them move you."

Miss Lemon's body went limp, and for a moment, Zoey wondered if the banker might slide right out of her chair.

"Well, I'd better get going." Zoey rose to her feet and straightened her toque. "I got a big day of cooking and baking ahead."

"Wait." Miss Lemon clutched her armrests to keep in her seat. "Is all your cooking this spectacular?"

"Yes," Zoey said.

Miss Lemon straightened her glasses. "How many blocks did you say it was to your house?"

What a Rush

 Zoey stood in front of a yellow stove-top oven, stirring a pot of bubbling hazelnut fudge. Steam rose like chimney smoke, fogging up the kitchen's windows and glass cupboards. Sweat dripped from Zoey's face, making her lips chapped and salty. Wiping her damp cheek on the shoulder of her jacket, Zoey thought to herself, *Someone should invent a toque with a mini air conditioner inside. Heaven knows there's room.*

She had four pots going at once. From the tallest of these pots emerged a wriggling octopus tentacle. Zoey whacked the tentacle with her red alder spoon. "Oh no you don't!" The tentacle slithered back into the pot.

Once again, Zoey plunged the spoon into the frothy fudge. While her right hand stirred, her left hand arranged five peeled bananas into a straight line on the counter. Then, the left hand caressed the handles of a dozen knives clinging to a magnetic strip on the wall. After a brief, tactile perusal, her fingers closed on the handle of a super-sharp, super-awesome, double-edged, rust-proof steel Misono 440

Santoku. *Yeah, baby.* With this prince of knives, her left hand commenced slicing the bananas into fat, symmetrical discs.

While her hands stirred and sliced, Zoey shimmied her right foot out of its boot. With her toes, she gripped one of the stove dials and turned it up to high heat. In the pot on the corresponding burner, four inches of oil, honey, and cinnamon bubbled to life. "They're coming, precious. They're coming."

Slipping her foot back into its boot, Zoey used the flat of her Santoku to scoop the banana slices into the pot. The oil hissed like an angry cobra as bubbles swarmed the bananas' flesh.

She tasted the fudge sauce. Milky. Nutty. Rich. A tad too runny, and that was deliberate. Chocolate sauce, you see, gets firmer as it cools. By the time her chocolate sauce reached a consumable temperature, the consistency would be just right.

Zoey ladled the fudge sauce into a small glass bowl. She placed the bowl on a silver platter, next to bowls of raspberry sauce and caramel sauce.

Next, she taste-tested a fried banana piece. Crunchy on the outside, gooey on the inside, yummy all over. *À la perfection.*

She plated the fried bananas, then plattered the plate. With steady hands, she carried the platter across the kitchen, toed open the two-way kitchen door, and glided into the dining room.

Miss Lemon sat at a baby-blue antique dining table, facing an open window with a panoramic view of San Francisco Bay.

Zoey balanced the platter against her hip. "So how are you loving it?"

"It's miraculous." Miss Lemon licked sauce off her fork. "I never thought pears and Parmesan would go together, but wow. And these pink rose petals, what a lovely aesthetic."

"*Merci.* Most people do a petal and ravioli in the same bite, but I prefer them separate. A rose's savor is delicate and nuanced. Doesn't play well with starch and cheese."

Miss Lemon gulped. "Oh, the petals are meant to be . . . *eaten?*"

"I put them on the plate, didn't I?"

Miss Lemon made an *I-really-don't-want-to-but-I-don't-wanna-hurt-your-feelings-either* face. (If you've ever tried to kiss someone who just wasn't that into you, you've seen it.)

"Go on," Zoey urged. "You'll love it."

With her fork, Miss Lemon scooped up a pink petal. She smelled it. She dabbed it with the tip of her tongue. She ate it. "Mm. That's tasty. Delicious, even."

"Wait until you try dessert." Zoey set the platter on the table. "*Voilà!* My Not-as-Famous-as-It-Should-Be-What's-the-Matter-with-You-People? Fried Banana Fondue. *Bon appétit.*"

Miss Lemon licked her fork clean and stabbed a banana slice. She plunged the banana into the hazelnut fudge sauce and spun the fork, causing the fudge to wrap around the banana like a hot blanket. She slid the confection into her mouth. "Holy wow! How did you . . . ? How can anything be this . . . ? Oh, that's divine."

Zoey curtseyed. "*Enchantée.* Back in a few."

In the kitchen again, Zoey replaced the fudge sauce pot with a taller pot full of water. *Now, where did those lobsters go?* Her eyes scanned the kitchen. A stack of banana leaves had fallen off the counter onto the floor. The leaves were moving.

"There you are!"

Zoey lifted the leaves, uncovering a pair of two-pound lobsters. She placed the lobsters into the pot of water on the stove. As the water heated to a boil, the lobsters thrashed and pinched, fighting to escape their bubbly death bath. The struggle was hard to watch, even for a seasoned chef like Zoey. This was the dark side of cooking. The side food journalists chose not to write about, and diners chose not to think about.

As the lobsters surrendered to the inevitable, Zoey thought she heard one cry out, "I never saw Paris. . . ."

Zoey whipped up a quick, creamy hollandaise sauce. She checked the lobsters (almost done). She laid thirty strips of Balinese Long Pepper Bacon on the countertop griddle and turned up the heat.

She yanked the octopus from its pot and plunked it down on the cutting board. With her super-awesome Santoku, she lopped off the octopus's tentacles, threw away the head (Americans won't eat heads), diced up the tentacles, and scooped the tentacle bits back into the pot.

To this pot she added salt and fresh-ground pepper, a halved onion, unpeeled ginger root, octopus bouillon cubes, anise stars, one Ceylon cinnamon stick, four scallions, one red jalapeño pepper, one green jalapeño pepper, fresh cilantro, Red Boat 40° N fish sauce (imported from Vietnam), and bean sprouts.

She glanced at the microwave clock. 11:56. *Better hurry.* She flipped the bacon on the griddle, poured a bag of banh pho rice noodles into the octopus pot, and swept into the dining room. "Noon is upon us, Miss Lemon. Let's get this loan wrapped up."

Miss Lemon touched a napkin to her lips. "Now, Zoey, I never agreed to approve your loan."

Zoey threw her hands up in disgust. "Unbelievable! I invite you into my home, I make you a delicious lunch, and you won't even lend me fifty thousand dollars. Are all your relationships this one-sided?"

"This isn't about lunch, Zoey. Mulberry Bank needs to see that you can turn your cooking into profit. You have to prove to us that you can bring in big money so we know you'll be able to pay back the loan."

The doorbell rang.

Zoey held a finger in the air. "Ah, the Lunch Rush."

"Lunch Rush?"

Zoey ran to the front door and pulled it open. About forty people stood in a line that began on Zoey's doorstep, snaked down the steep and lengthy porch stairway, and ended on the slanted sidewalk.

First in line was a tall hulk of a man with a bald head and bushy black beard. He wore greasy black jeans and a black leather vest. Tattoos of motorcycles, skeletons, and fanged clowns decorated his muscular arms, shoulders, and chest.

"*Bonjour*, Knuckles," Zoey said. "How's the gang?"

"Ridin' hard, ridin' fast," Knuckles said. His voice sounded like a rock being dragged over a cheese grater. "Jus' got back from a road trip t' Reno. Had a nasty run-in with the cops there. Turns out it's against the law to ride a Harley inside a casino. Who knew?" He sniffed. "The specials?"

"Lobster Eggs Benedict and Cinnamon Bacon Octopus Pho."

"Pho me."

"*Un moment.*" Zoey zipped into the kitchen. She returned a minute later with a bulky pink paper bag.

Knuckles took the bag, opened the top, and sniffed. "Smells wicked." He handed Zoey a wad of dollar bills and walked away.

A policeman was next in line.

"*Bonjour*, Officer Haggis. This is, what, six Saturdays in a row for you now?"

"Eh, who's counting? Say, ya got any of them Chocolate-Covered Pork Chops?"

"None today. I get my cocoa beans from a grower in India. His latest shipment was delayed due to flash floods in Punjab. They'll get here in the next day or two."

"Ah, the old floods-in-Punjab alibi. I've used it a few times myself. Almost got me out of paying for my daughter's wedding."

"Lobster Eggs Benedict or Cinnamon Bacon Octopus Pho?"

"I never say no to lobster."

"*Un moment.*" Zoey flitted into the kitchen and emerged a minute later with another pink paper bag. "*Voilà.*"

Officer Haggis accepted the bag and handed Zoey a crisp twenty-dollar bill. "See ya next Saturday, Chef."

For the next hour, Zoey hustled back and forth between the kitchen and the front door, handing out pink bags of awesomeness and taking people's money. When the hour was over and the last customer had been served, Zoey closed the front door and sighed. "That was fun."

Miss Lemon laid her fork on her empty plate. "Chef, how much money did you make today?"

Zoey reached into her pockets and pulled out two fat wads of cash. "About this much."

Miss Lemon twiddled her fingers. "May I count it?"

"Be my guest." Zoey walked over and laid the cash on the table.

Miss Lemon licked her fingertips and counted the dollar bills. "I don't believe it. You made twelve hundred dollars in one hour."

Zoey smirked. "I guess this proves I can bring in big money."

"Indeed."

Zoey's heart raced. "Are you saying . . . ?"

"I am saying that Mulberry Bank will be delighted to lend you fifty thousand dollars."

Zoey threw her hands in the air and shrieked. "Holy hopping hotcakes! I'm opening a restaurant!"

Miss Lemon stood and hung her purse on one shoulder. "Come to my office on Monday morning. I'll have the loan agreement ready for you to sign. Bring your parents. They must sign as well."

Zoey gulped. "My . . . *parents* . . . have to sign?"

"Yes."

"But I'm the one getting the loan."

"You're a minor. We cannot lend money to a minor unless the minor's parents assume co-liability."

"Koala-what?"

"It means if you fail to repay the loan, your parents have to."

Uh-oh. "My parents can't make it Monday. They're, uh, in Siberia."

"I thought they were at work."

"They . . . *are.* They work there."

"Your parents work in Siberia?"

"Yes."

"Doing what?"

"Oh, you know . . ." *Think, Zoey, think.* ". . . raising llamas."

"Llamas?"

Oh boy. "Yep, llamas."

"In Siberia?"

"You know what they say: Siberians love llamas."

"Your parents left you here alone?"

"Yep. They told me, 'Zoey, you stay here and open a restaurant, and we support you a hundred and ten percent, and if Mulberry Bank wants us to cosign something, you have our express permission to sign on our behalf. Because we're in Siberia. With llamas.'"

Miss Lemon dove into her purse. "I'm calling Child Protective Services."

"Wait, did you say *Monday?*" Zoey gave a nervous giggle. "Monday is great. I'll be there. My parents will be there. Our neighbors might even come. Hey, do you like homemade ice cream?"

Forty minutes and two bowls of Pistachio Pumpkin Gelato later, Zoey stood on her front porch, watching a taxi carry Miss Lemon away. She felt happy, but also uneasy.

She had persuaded a major bank to lend her fifty thousand dollars, sure, but now she had an even bigger mountain to climb.

She had to persuade her mother.

Walking the Garbage

 Zoey's mom wasn't hip to the whole Lunch Rush thing. "It's unwise," she had said, "my young daughter home alone, all kinds of strangers stopping by: too dangerous."

Initially, Zoey's dad had supported the Lunch Rush. But, like all good husbands, he lived in mortal fear of upsetting his woman. ("Happy wife equals happy life," he liked to say.) So Zoey's mom got her way on the matter. (Or so she thought.)

The house rule was clear: Zoey was not, under any circumstances, to sell her culinary delights to a Lunch Rush, or a Dinner Rush, or any other Rush that involved strangers coming to the house. That's why, as Zoey hurried about the kitchen, sweeping up this and wiping down that, she wasn't just cleaning—she was disposing of evidence.

She soaked and scrubbed and rinsed and dried until every dish, utensil, appliance, and surface was sparkling clean. Exhausted but invigorated, she leaned against the fridge and massaged her sore hands. If only dishes were as fun to clean as they were to make dirty.

All that remained of the Lunch Rush was a big black

garbage bag leaning against the pantry door, bulging like a baby's diaper after a long nap. The bag was too big to put in the cans in the garage (her mom would see, get suspicious, ask questions) and too heavy to carry all the way to the Dumpster behind the Starbucks on Bay Street. She needed an alternative means of disposal.

The doorbell rang.

Zoey dragged the garbage bag to the front room and opened the door. On the porch stood a pimple-faced boy in a Pizza Town hat, cradling a red pizza warmer.

Zoey did her best to look surprised. "Pizza? I didn't order pizza."

The pizza boy checked the receipt on his pizza warmer. "Is this 816 Francisco Street?"

"That's my address, but I didn't order pizza."

The pizza boy made a *great-I-came-all-this-way-for-nothing* face. (If you've ever handed out toothbrushes to trick-or-treaters on Halloween, you've seen it.) "I guess I'll . . . go, then. . . ."

"Tell you what." Zoey slid the garbage bag to the doorstep. "If you'll take this bag off my hands, I'll buy that pizza and give you a ten-dollar tip."

The pizza boy looked elated. Then suspicious. "What's in the bag?"

"Leftovers."

"That's not, like, a code word for 'dead body,' is it? Because the last time I accepted a bulging black bag from a stranger I ended up in juvie."

"It's just garbage, I assure you. Do we have a deal or not?"

The pizza boy glanced over his shoulder. "Are you filming me?"

"You have three seconds to decide. Three."

With his free hand, the pizza boy took off his cap, scratched his bushy purple mohawk with the back of his wrist. "Make it twenty?"

"No. Two."

He put the cap back on. "I'd better not."

"One. You snooze, you lose." Zoey slammed the door shut. She dug thirty dollars out of her pocket, and waited. *One soda pop, two soda pop, three soda pop,* now.

The doorbell rang.

Zoey opened the door. "That's more like it." She paid the pizza boy and took the pizza. The pizza boy lugged the garbage bag to a dilapidated Honda Civic parked at the curb, threw it in the backseat, and drove away.

Zoey locked up the house and marched down the street, hot pizza box in hand. The sky was blue. The air was warm. Seagulls soared overhead, riding the salty Pacific wind, squawking like old women at a Marie Callender's.

Turning onto Hyde Street, Zoey got a clear view of the bay. The sea was choppy. Whitecaps twinkled in the sun. Yachts and sailboats drifted past Alcatraz Island, site of America's most famous prison, and former residence of notorious gangsters like Al Capone, Clint Eastwood, and that one guy who was way too into birds.

To the west, the orange-red Golden Gate Bridge loomed over the Pacific strait like a sentinel. The bridge was in pretty good shape, considering its history. If you've watched any movies in the past five decades, you've seen the bridge fall prey to numerous attacks. Assailants include a giant shark, the Incredible Hulk, an army of hyper-intelligent apes, Magneto, Godzilla, something called a "*kaijū*," the sun, the cast of *Full House*, and Lex Luthor. Yes, *that* Lex Luthor.

Zoey removed her toque, letting the breeze rake through her cheesecake-colored hair like a velvet fork. Such a lovely afternoon. Had she not been so nervous, she might've enjoyed it.

Crossing Bay Street, she heard the distant *tah-tah-tu-tah-tah* of a stick on a ride cymbal and the sassy honk of a brass trumpet.

She swallowed the lump in her throat.

Valentine & the Night Owls

 The Jam House was the smallest house on Bret Harte Terrace, salmon with a teal front door and Spanish-tile steps. Ascending the steps, Zoey's heart thumped like a kick drum. *Breathe, Zoey, breathe.* She didn't bother with the doorbell. They wouldn't have heard her anyway. She let herself in.

Valentine & the Night Owls were in the living room performing the final refrains of Charlie Parker's bebop classic "Scrapple from the Apple." Fat Jo sat behind a Gretsch drum kit, satin walnut with brass rims. Monk sat at an upright piano. Four stood behind an upright bass. Bird stood next to Four, clutching a copper tenor saxophone.

Zoey's mom stood at the center of the room, a beret on her pretty head, a black scarf around her long white neck, a brass trumpet held to her lips, her cheeks puffed up like balloons. Her name was Suzy but everyone called her Valentine—a nod to her favorite song, "My Funny Valentine," as performed by Chet Baker.

Zoey's dad sat on a barstool in the back corner of the room. His name was Kenny, but everyone called him

Gershwin because he, like the late George Gershwin, was such a skilled composer. He managed the quintet (bookings, press, accounting, etc.) and composed or arranged every piece in its 200-plus song repertoire. Gershwin, in spite of his Anglo-Californian roots, always dressed like a Cuban cigar tycoon. Today's outfit was a panama hat (handwoven toquilla palm with a black band and beach-style brim), a white suit, lime-green collared shirt, and white-and-beige wingtip shoes. His reason for this fashion choice: "If a millionaire ever invites me to brunch on his yacht, I'll be ready."

An open book of scores lay on Gershwin's lap. His eyes followed the score while his left hand carved a 4/4 pattern into the air, in time with the band.

The room smelled like black coffee and Fat Jo's unwashed pit bull, Pistachio. The mutt was likely upstairs in her room, head on the floor, paws over her ears. She hated jazz.

One by one, the members of Valentine & the Night Owls greeted Zoey with a smile or nod. They hammed up their performances because that's what musicians do when someone's watching. Bird raised his sax and swayed his hips. Monk bobbed his head and shoulders. Four pursed his lips and slapped his strings. Valentine teased a mute in and out of her trumpet's bell, producing a *wah-wah* effect that sounded like catfish gumbo tastes.

At the conclusion of a zippy cadence, Fat Jo clenched the rim of his Meinl crash, squelching the sound. "Wuttup, Lil Z."

"*Bonjour*, fellas, Mom, Dad. I brought you a pizza."

Fat Jo received the box and took out a slice of thin-crust

pepperoni. "Thass what I'm talkin' 'bout." He handed the box to Four and Bird, who took slices for themselves, then passed the box to Monk.

Valentine plucked a white handkerchief from her back pocket and rubbed it over her trumpet's bell, wiping off the spit spots. "I can't remember the last time you came to a rehearsal, sweetie. Is everything okay?"

"Yep, everything's great. Just popping in to see the world's coolest mom doing her thing." Zoey twiddled her fingers in front of her mouth to mimic playing a trumpet. Zoey's parents exchanged cynical glances. Valentine said to Zoey, "You burned down the house, didn't you?"

"What? No."

"Invited a drifter to live in our attic?"

"That was an isolated incident."

Gershwin set down his book of scores. "Is PETA harassing you again?"

"Nothing like that. Everything is fine. Really." Zoey sniffed. "Hey, I ran out of *mitsuba*. Tomorrow morning, can you and Dad give me a ride to Nijiya Market?"

"Sure, sweetie," Valentine said. "Is that it?"

"That's it." Zoey dawdled at the front door. "That's all I came for. No ulterior motives whatsoever." She opened the door and stepped outside, adding, "On the way to Nijiya, we'll swing by Mulberry Bank to cosign my business loan. Bye!"

She ran for it.

"*Stop.*"

Zoey stopped. She'd made it halfway down the Spanish-tile steps. The door hadn't even closed all the way yet.

"Inside. Now."

Zoey went back inside.

Gershwin and the Night Owls were grinning like house-husbands at a taping of *The Rachael Ray Show*.

Valentine, however, was less than amused. "Business loan?"

"I'm opening a restaurant."

Gershwin gave two thumbs up. "Attagirl!"

Valentine elbowed him in the ribs. "Don't encourage her. Zoey, how much?"

"The number isn't important. What's important is your daughter is pursuing her dreams."

Valentine folded her arms, her trumpet against her ribs. "How much?"

"Fifty."

"Fifty what?"

"Fifty . . . *ish*."

"How much is *ish*?"

"I don't remember the exact number."

Valentine put her foot down. Literally. Her French heel struck the hardwood floor like a judge's gavel. "*Zoey Sara Lee Kate.*"

Zoey mumbled, "Fifty thousand."

Fat Jo played a drumroll on his snare. "Daaang, the girl takes care o' biz-ness!"

Monk said, "That's almost as much as I owe the IRS."

Four said, "I get so lonely sometimes."

Bird said, "I'm staying out of this."

"So, Mom, Dad, will you cosign?"

"Absolutely not," Valentine said. "Fifty thousand dollars is too much of a liability. Isn't that right, Gersh?"

Gershwin stuck his hands into his pockets and shrugged.

"Actually, wife dearest, I think the restaurant is a brilliant idea. Also, you're beautiful and thin and I love you."

Fat Jo said, "I dig it."

Monk said, "Me too."

Four said, "I just want someone to love me for me, you know?"

Bird said, "I'm staying out of this."

Zoey said, "Mom, everyone else thinks it's a good idea. Why don't you?"

"You're twelve," Valentine said.

"That's ageism!"

"What about school?"

"It's summer."

"Won't be summer forever."

"When school starts, I'll do the school thing during the week. I'll do the restaurant thing on weekends."

"What about friends?"

Zoey blushed. She didn't have any friends, and she was pretty darn sure her mom knew that. No point bringing it up in front of the band.

Noticing her hesitation, Valentine said, "What about Dallin?"

Oh, well, yeah, there was Dallin. But he wasn't a friend, per se. He was more like . . . a brother? No, he was too dependable for that. More like . . . a piece of furniture. An old couch, perhaps. Big, fluffy, comfortable, always had her back.

"I got big plans for him," Zoey said. "I'll start him bussing tables, then serving. If he performs well, by autumn he could be managing the front of house. I'll know more after his first performance review."

Valentine fired an ominous look at Gershwin, who was smiling. And then, suddenly, not smiling.

"And your father and I, when will we see you?"

"Your band gigs six nights a week! I won't see you any less than I do now."

Valentine flinched as if an invisible bee had stung her below the left eye. Zoey hadn't intended the comment to hurt, but it had.

"What about safety?" Valentine said. "Dad and I will be on one side of town, doing a gig, and you'll be all the way on the other side of town, cooking. How will we know you're safe?"

"I'll hire Navy SEALs to wait tables."

Valentine shook her head. "I'm uncomfortable with this whole thing."

Gershwin coughed into his fist. *"How ban."*

Fat Jo said, "Gesundheit."

Gershwin coughed into his fist again. *"Howz bad."*

Valentine said, "Cough drops are in my purse in the kitchen."

Gershwin looked at Zoey like, *Are you kidding me?* then coughed into his fist again. *"Hows ban."*

"House band!" Zoey shouted, finally getting it.

Valentine shot an ominous look at her husband. He pretended to study something interesting on the ceiling.

"The quintet can be my house band," Zoey said. "You'll get to perform for a packed house every night, and, Mom, you can keep a close eye on me. Closer than you get to now."

Fat Jo said, "I'm in."

Monk said, "Me too."

Four said, "My heart is a desolate wasteland."

Bird said, "I'm staying out of this."

Gershwin placed a hand on his wife's shoulder. "Babe, you've already outlawed the Lunch Rush. What else is Zoey supposed to do?"

Valentine looked down at her trumpet. Her agile fingers played a silent tune on the keys. She appeared deep in thought. Was she reconsidering?

"I still say no."

Nope. Not reconsidering.

Fat Jo whacked his crash cymbal. The copper *PAHHHH!* rippled through the room like an EMP blast, making everyone jump. "Aw, come on, Val! Cosign the girl's loan. Let her chase her dreams. Where would you be with that trumpet of yours if your parents hadn't sneaked you into all them jazz clubs when you was a kid? You only live once, right?"

Gershwin said, "He's got a point, babe."

Monk said, "I agree."

Four said, "A man can only read so many Nicholas Sparks novels, ya know?"

Bird said, "I'm still staying out of this, but if I wasn't I'd say 'me too' too."

You only live once, Zoey thought, committing the phrase to memory. *So obvious yet so profound.*

Valentine's fingers played another silent lick on the trumpet's keys. Her foot tapped on the hardwood floor. "Zoey, do you promise you won't fall behind in school?"

"I promise."

"And do you promise you won't do anything foolish

or dangerous as you're getting your restaurant up and running?"

"Cross my heart and hope to eat meat loaf."

Valentine nodded, her face as brittle as an overcooked crêpe. "Fine, I'll cosign."

Zoey threw her hands in the air. Gershwin pumped his fists. Fat Jo played a rollicking drum fill, and the band—minus its lead trumpeter—launched into a spirited rendition of "The Best Is Yet to Come."

Details, Schmetails

Zoey sat in the backseat of her family's gray Highlander, flipping through her crisp new Mulberry Bank checkbook and feeling like a millionaire. (Or a fifty-thousand-dollar-ionaire. Is that a thing?)

Her mom sat in the passenger seat. She stared out the window, looking grim and mournful, like she'd come from a funeral. (The black dress and veil didn't help.)

Her dad drove. He kept trying to cheer up his wife, saying things like, "That Miss Lemon was a nice gal," and "I love Monday mornings, don't you, dear?" but Valentine was beyond cheering up.

Turning onto Bay Street, Gershwin said, "Hey, Chef, where is your restaurant going to be, anyway?"

"My real estate agent texted me addresses of several properties available for rent. He wants me to swing by each one, peek through the windows, get a feel for the neighborhood, kick the proverbial tires. If any of the properties pique my interest, he'll make arrangements for a walk-through."

Gershwin's eyes darted to the rearview mirror. "When did you get a real estate agent?"

"A few weeks ago. Found him online."

Valentine shook her head. "What else don't we know about our daughter's life?"

Zoey put her new checkbook in her tangerine purse. "So, itinerary: first, brunch at Café Bastille. Smoked salmon benedict and Orangina. Then cruise around town, check out some properties, see what catches my eye. Then dinner. La Cucina di Cannoli. Spaghetti and meatballs, old-school. I'll take the Powell/Hyde home. You two will head to tonight's gig. Is this an awesome day or what?"

"We can't," Valentine said. "Gig this afternoon."

"Since when does the quintet do afternoon gigs? Your fan base is nocturnal."

Gershwin eased off the gas pedal to turn onto Hyde Street. "The Boom Boom Room needed a fill-in. We said we'd do it. The soonest we can take you is Saturday morning."

"I'll be an old woman by then!" Zoey folded her arms and stared out the window, doing her best to look down-trodden so her parents would see how cruel they were being. "You two are standing in the way of progress."

"Saturday," Gershwin said, "take it or leave it."

"Leave it," Zoey said. "Time waits for no chef!"

"Suit yourself," Valentine said.

Zoey would have to go it alone. She'd take taxis and cable cars and even the city bus. Since public transportation was a weirdo-magnet, Zoey would need protection—someone tough and loyal whom she could count on to watch her back.

She knew just the guy.

The Boy Behind the Sleds

 Football camp was every weekday from nine to noon at Moscone Park. Zoey sat in the shade of a Spanish chestnut tree, watching a gaggle of preteen boys in helmets and shoulder pads pummel one another. Often, a pointy brown ball was involved.

Zoey (who looked resplendent in her banana-yellow toque and jacket) scanned the grubby throng in search of Dallin Caraway. Dallin was the biggest kid on the team, so he should've been easy to spot. But Zoey couldn't find him. Where was he?

At noon, the coach blew a whistle and called the boys "a buncha thumb-suckin' mamas' boys," signaling the end of practice.

As the haggard players limped off the field, Zoey approached the coach. "Excuse me. I'm looking for Dallin Caraway . . . ?"

The coach motioned to the other end of the park. "Over there. Blocking sleds."

Zoey could see the sleds but she didn't see Dallin. "Are you sure he's—"

"Trust me. He's there."

Zoey scurried to the other end of the park. As she neared the sled, she spotted a red mesh sleeve poking out from behind one of the blocking pads.

"Dal, is that you?"

The sleeve vanished.

"Dal, I saw your sleeve."

No response.

Zoey walked around the blocking sled. There was Dallin, in his helmet, shoulder pads, and sweatpants, crouching like a frightened mouse. (A *big* frightened mouse.)

"Worst. Hiding spot. Ever," Zoey said.

Dallin rose to his feet. He was the height and width of a refrigerator: half muscle, half baby fat, all boy. Behind his face mask, his cheeks were redder than cherries jubilee. "What're you doing here, Z?"

"I'm about to make history, and I need your help. Why were you hiding from me?"

Dallin ripped off his helmet and threw it to the ground. His brown hair was a sweaty mess. Clumps of grass and dirt clung to his broad chin and neck. "You weren't supposed to see me like this."

"Like what?"

Dallin kicked his helmet. It flew six feet, landing on a patch of wild dandelions. "Coach says for a lineman I don't hit hard enough. He makes me spend every practice hitting this stupid blocking sled."

Zoey wondered how it was possible that a boy of Dallin's size could come up short in the hit-hard department. But that was a mystery for another time. Dallin was sad, and it was her job to cheer him up. Fortunately, she knew the perfect thing to say:

"Hang in there, Dal. A lot of great athletes have bumpy starts. When Babe Ruth joined the Chicago Bulls in 1982, Coach Lombardi said he was too fat to play goalie. Did the Babe give up? No, sirree. He hired a personal trainer, beat cancer, and in the summer of '69 became the first Mexican American to win six Tour de Frances."

Dallin was speechless.

The pep talk had worked, obviously. Dallin was all cheered up, and it was time for business. "Here's one for ya," she said. "What's cute and brilliant and is starting her own restaurant?"

Dallin said, "You got the loan?"

"Fifty g's, baby."

"Suh-weet!"

They bumped fists.

"You're gonna help me find the perfect property for my restaurant. We'll head out as soon as you're cleaned up."

"Um, okay." In one motion, Dallin tore off his jersey and shoulder pads. They hit the ground like a sack of Klondike Rose potatoes. "Ready."

Zoey surveyed Dallin's outfit: faded 49ers T-shirt with pit stains, black sweats with holes in the knees, and tomato-red cleats. Her disapproval must've shown on her face, because Dallin said, "What?"

Zoey said, "Don't you have a change of clothes somewhere?"

Dallin said, "You're looking at it."

"We might meet someone important today. You should look fashionable."

"Oh, right." Dallin rubbed his hand through his hair, whipping up a cloud of dust. He pressed a sooty finger against his right nostril and blew a wad of dirty snot out of his left. "How's this?"

Zoey chuckled and shook her head. "As good as it's gonna get, I suppose. Let's go."

The California Line

 California Street was long and steep. Narrow row houses, four and five stories tall, stood close together like tattered books on slanted shelves. Some of the houses had bars on the windows. Most did not. Fire escapes zigzagged down the fronts of hotels and apartment towers. Here and there, residents sat in folding chairs on fire escape landings, sipping cola drinks, watching the traffic, killing time, waiting for an adorable young chef to open a restaurant already.

A cable car glided eastward, slow and steady like a reggae song. Zoey and Dallin sat in the back of this car. Dallin was hunched over a two-pound pepperoni-and-cheddar mega hoagie like a greedy gorilla. Zoey was on her iPad, reading restaurant reviews and ignoring the gawking stares of her fellow passengers.

For the unacquainted, a cable car is an open-air boxcar that looks like an old-fashioned train caboose. It has no wheels. It links to (you guessed it) a cable underground that pulls the car up and down a defined route called a "line."

San Francisco has three lines: the Powell/Hyde Line, which runs by Zoey's house; the Powell/Mason Line; and the California Line. (Fun fact: country music legend Johnny Cash wrote the song "I Walk the Line" after getting kicked off a cable car for disorderly conduct.)

With grease dribbling down his chin, Dallin looked at Zoey's iPad and said, "Who's the dork?"

On-screen was a photo of a middle-aged man with glossy pecan-colored hair and a handlebar mustache that curled upward at both ends. He wore a black three-piece suit with a gold watch chain tucked into the vest pockets. He was fat.

"That," Zoey said, "is Royston Basil Boarhead, *Golden Gate Magazine*'s editor in chief and California's most esteemed food critic."

"Never heard of him," Dallin said.

"That's because he's not a football player. He's the most powerful man in gastronomic journalism. With a stroke of his pen, he can make or break any restaurant. Remember the Coddled Egg on Fillmore?"

"No."

"Exactly. Three years ago, Boarhead published a review titled 'The Coddled Egg Is a Rotten Egg.' Five days later, the restaurant was out of business."

"Hard-core."

"Way."

Dallin tore off a chunk of cheesy pepperoni with his teeth. "So is every chef in town, like, terrified of cooking for him?"

"*Au contraire.*" Zoey slid the iPad into her purse. "It's an honor to cook for Boarhead. He has the most discerning palate in North America. He can eat a potato and tell you what part of Idaho it's from."

"Whoa."

"Yeah."

Dallin licked a gob of cheddar off the side of his palm. "When your restaurant gets open, will you get to cook for him?"

"I can only hope."

The cable car stopped at a red light at Mason Street. Zoey's eyes panned up the towering InterContinental Mark Hopkins hotel. The top floor, Zoey knew, was a posh cocktail bar called Top of the Mark. Now there was a cool place for a restaurant. Too bad the space was wasted on something as vulgar and uninspiring as cocktails. Zoey made a mental note to contact Mark Hopkins (whoever he was) and offer her services as a consulting chef should he ever wise up and turn that bar into a gourmet steak house.

Dallin said, "Whatcha gonna call it, anyway?"

"Call what?"

"Your restaurant, duh."

"Oh." Excitement coursed up Zoey's spine, causing her to sit up straight. "I've given this a lot of thought. A restaurant name has to pop and sizzle without undermining its own potential for socioeconomic change. For example, when people eat at my restaurant, they'll get inspired. This will lead them to invent things and start mega-successful companies with thousands of employees. So I'm a job creator. The name has to reflect that.

"Also, my restaurant will facilitate a lot of love connections. Picture a young couple on their first date, rapturously enjoying my food, their emotions running as wild as African antelopes. The guy says, 'Wow, I am loving this.' The girl thinks, 'Wait, is he loving the food or loving our date? I wonder how many kids he wants.'

"Then the guy looks deep into the girl's eyes and says, 'Will you—'

"'A thousand times yes!' she exclaims. Actually, he was going to ask her to pass the butter, but it's too late. She already told her family and bought a dress. They'll be married this autumn. I'll cater. I bring families together. The name must reflect that too."

Dallin bit into a thread of cheese dangling from his hoagie. "That's why I never talk while eating."

"Also," Zoey said, "a lot of world leaders will eat at my restaurant. Senators, presidents, czars, kings, that kind of thing. One guy will be like, 'If you people don't stop flying into our airspace, we'll drop a bomb on you.' And another guy will be like, 'If you drop a bomb on us, we'll invade your country.' And another guy will be like, 'Wow, these Cajun Gumbo Tacos are amazing!' And the first two guys will be like, 'Who can fight at a time like this?' Boom. World War Three averted. I'm an ambassador for peace. The name has to reflect that too."

Dallin picked a speck of cheese out of his nostril. "So, what is it?"

"The name is . . ." Zoey drummed her hands on her thighs. ". . . Wait for it . . ." She pulled a fistful of confetti from her purse and flung it into the air. *"The Z Connection!"*

As glittery bits of paper rained on the heads and shoulders of nearby passengers, Dallin said, "How long have you been carrying that around?"

"Eight weeks. Did you like it?"

Dallin whiffled confetti off the top of his hoagie. "It's kinda messy."

"I meant the name. Did you like it?"

"Sure."

"You hate it."

"I didn't say that."

"I can tell."

Across the aisle, an old man brushed confetti off the shoulders of his wool cardigan, grumbling about "kids these days" and "not enough juvenile detention centers."

Zoey said, "You should see it written down. There's an exclamation mark at the end. It adds a lot."

"Ya know what I don't get?" Dallin said. "The Olive Garden. I've been there. No olives. No garden. Who're they trying to fool?"

"I have other names," Zoey said. "Zoey's Edible Arts?"

Dallin frowned. "Makes me picture a guy walking around a museum, licking all the paintings."

"That's creepy, but okay. How about . . . Zoey's Bistro?"

"Too generic."

"Zoey's Super-Fantastic Dazzling Delectables?"

"Too braggy."

"Eat Here or Your Mother Will Die."

"Too soon."

"La Cuisine de Nuit."

"Too French."

"Wolfgang Puck Is a Milksop."

"Too Wolfgang-y."

Zoey slouched like a deflated bicycle tire. "I got nuthin'."

"You should call it . . ." Dallin moved his hands in a sweeping motion, as if unveiling something grand and spectacular. "Because You Don't Feel Like Cooking, Anyway."

"Worst name ever."

"Or . . ." Dallin did the sweeping-hands motion again. "It's Either This or Your Wife's Cooking."

The old man in the cardigan grumbled something about "lousy wife" and "can't make a proper lasagna" and "why, I oughta . . ."

The light turned green. The cable car resumed its eastward trek. As they neared Grant Avenue, Zoey sprang to her feet. "This is us."

Dallin licked cheddar off his chin. "*Kiatow?*" (That was Dallin-with-his-mouth-full for "Chinatown?")

"It's the first address on my list."

"*Yu nah ky-nese.*" ("You're not Chinese.")

"You don't have to be Chinese to work in Chinatown. All kinds of people work there: Japanese, Korean, vegan . . ."

As the cable car slowed to a stop, a look of alarm swept across Dallin's face.

Zoey said, "What's wrong?"

"My hoagie. There's eight inches left."

"So take it with you."

"I can't start a meal in one place and finish it in another place. It'll freak out my digestive system."

The cable car conductor turned in his seat. "Yo, kid, you stayin' or leavin'?"

Panicked, Dallin looked at the conductor, then at the sidewalk, then at his hoagie. "Idea."

He closed his eyes. He opened his mouth wide. He held

the hoagie to his lips, then pushed. The first six inches went in no problem. The final two inches went in by force.

He chewed.

He swallowed.

A hoagie-shaped bulge appeared below his jaw, moved down his neck, and disappeared below his shoulders. It was like watching a python swallow a rabbit. It was disgusting and horrible and painful to watch. And yet . . . *beautiful* too.

But mostly horrible.

Zoey and Dallin hopped off the cable car (well, Zoey hopped; Dallin sort of hobbled) and started up Grant Avenue.

Chinatown

 Grant Avenue was a terrible name for Grant Avenue. It deserved a more fitting name, like China Avenue, or Dragon Avenue, or You Are No Longer in America You Better Have a Visa Avenue.

Buildings had curved pagoda roofs with turquoise tiles. Chinese characters festooned storefronts, marquees, and balconies. Red paper lanterns hung over the street like banners. Statues of dragons with curved claws and teeth clung to lampposts and store signs. Skinned pigs and ducks and frogs, their heads and teeth and feet still attached, hung in storefront windows like the lollipops at Ghirardelli Square.

Zoey and Dallin tromped up the sidewalk, counting the numbers on buildings—". . . 204 . . . 208 . . . 214 . . ."— working their way toward 568 Grant Avenue.

They passed a seafood shop. The day's catch was on display, open-market-style. Whole salmons, sturgeons, flounders, and other deep-sea goodies lay in rows on a bed of melting ice cubes, scales glinting in the afternoon sun.

Dallin pinched his nose. "This place reeks."

"What's the matter, Dal, you don't like fish?"

"I like it when you make it. When you make it, it doesn't smell like this."

They passed an old man in a bamboo cone hat peddling deep-fried scorpion shish kebabs.

"Good snack, yes?" the old man said. "You buy two, yes?"

Dallin dismissed the offer with a wave. "I prefer to live, thanks."

"Two for price of one, yes?" the old man said.

"Another time," Zoey said. One day, she would eat scorpion shish kebabs. She would be in China, at Beijing's famous Night Market, where she'd eat all kinds of creepy-crawly goodies: grasshoppers, centipedes, silkworm cocoons, sea horses, and, yes, deep-fried scorpions on a stick. (The deep-fry neutralizes the poison in the stingers, rendering them safe to eat.) Eating scorpions in faraway China was exciting and adventurous. But eating scorpions in California, two miles from one's own house: that's like sneaking into the lions' den at the zoo because "Hey, those African safaris sure look fun!" Some things should only be done in foreign countries.

The old man muttered something under his breath. Zoey didn't catch it, but his frosty tone gave her the willies.

Dallin said, "If anyone messes with us, get behind me. Got it?"

"Yeah."

They passed a martial arts studio with big windows. Inside, three teenage girls were kicking a mannequin like it owed them money.

"Speaking of which," Dallin said (which was weird

because they hadn't been speaking of anything), "did you know Bruce Lee was born in San Francisco?"

Zoey said, "Who's Bruce Lee?"

"Oh, come on. Bruce Lee. The greatest kung fu fighter of all time. How have you never heard of Bruce Lee?"

"I don't follow kung fu, okay?"

"Yeah but . . . it's *Bruce Lee*. Everyone knows Bruce Lee."

"Tell me," Zoey said, aiming to give Dallin a taste of his own margarine, "who is Marco Pierre White?"

"He discovered America."

"Nope."

"Discovered malaria?"

"He's the godfather of modern cooking."

"Oh, *Marco* Pierre White. I thought you said *Axl* Pierre White."

"I believe the word you're looking for is 'touché.'" Zoey licked her thumb, then wiped a smear of cheddar off Dallin's round left cheek. "He was the youngest chef ever to win three Michelin stars."

"Only three, huh?"

"Not *only* three. Three is the max. The top of the mountain. La crème de la crème. It's the most prestigious cooking award in the world."

"Hold on." Dallin stopped. "Michelin, as in the tire people?"

Zoey stopped. "Michelin makes tires?"

"Haven't you seen the Michelin Man? He's made of tires."

"Oh. I thought those were marshmallows."

They resumed their trek up Grant Avenue. After a brief

stop for some scallion pancakes (somehow, Dallin was hungry again), they arrived at 568 Grant Avenue. They pressed their noses against the window, cupped their hands around the sides of their faces, and peered inside.

"It's not much to look at," Dallin said.

"That's because there's nothing in it," Zoey said.

"I don't like the color."

"I'll change the color."

"Is that a chalk outline?"

"I'll have the floor tiled."

"I got a bad feeling about this one, Z."

"I'll take it!"

Zoey whipped out her iPhone. Dialing her real estate agent, she leaned her back against 568's window. There came a break in the flow of cars on the street, and that's when she saw it. She ended the call. "Dal, look!"

"Wow. A building."

"It's New Shanghai!"

"What'd you call me?"

"It's Chef Pao's restaurant."

"Who?"

"Chef Pao, the most acclaimed chef in San Francisco." Putting her phone back in her skirt pocket, Zoey racked her brain for a way to make Dallin understand what a huge deal this was. "Dal, who's your favorite 49er of all time?"

"Justin Smith, aka 'the Cowboy,' starting defensive end, two-double-o-eight to twenty-fourteen, two-time 49ers MVP, *Sports Illustrated* Defensive Player of the Year in twenty-eleven, five Pro Bowls, and eighty-seven career QB sacks. Justin Smith lives in Missouri with his lovely wife and two children."

"Well, Chef Pao . . ." Zoey pointed at New Shanghai. ". . . is my Justin Smith."

Dallin's jaw dropped. "Whoa."

Zoey bounced up and down like a pogo stick. "Sweet banana cream pie! I'm going to work across the street from Chef Pao! We'll be professional acquaintances! We'll chitchat after work! Swap kitchen war stories! Carpool to award shows! This is epic! I have to meet him. Come on!"

She grabbed Dallin by the hand and darted into the street.

The Golden Toque

 If the dude who designed New Shanghai's foyer had intended to make visitors feel welcome, he'd failed big-time. There were no windows. The walls, floor, and ceiling were stone. Candle lanterns, perched on tiny alcoves, provided the room's only light. Massive double doors, red with gold studs, separated the foyer from the restaurant proper like the gates of the Forbidden City.

Dallin scratched the top of his head. "Where is everybody?"

"It's reservation-only," Zoey said. "Obviously, no one has a reservation for this very second, so the hostess doesn't have to be out here."

"Should we knock on those red doors?"

"We're not marauders. We'll hang out. I'm sure someone will come."

Dallin wandered off to a corner to admire a seven-foot statue of an ancient Chinese warrior. "Cool. Samurai."

"Samurai are Japanese. That's a Terracotta Warrior."

"You sure? Because this thing looks like a samurai. Helmet. Armor. Sword. Fu Manchu."

"I'm sure."

Zoey looked around for a place to sit and spotted a glimmering glass trophy case. The case was stationed against the same wall as the front door so folks wouldn't see it when they first walked in, but on the way out they couldn't miss it. A savvy move on Chef Pao's part. Had the trophy case been the focal point of the room, Chef Pao would've come off as braggy. At its current station, however, it was an afterthought, an oh-by-the-way, a PS at the end of a well-crafted letter.

PS: You just ate the best meal of your life. Everything after this will be huge disappointment.

Zoey moved in for a closer look. There were Michelin stars, James Beard Awards, Silver Spoon Awards, a Most Likely to Beat Up a Food Critic Award (turns out that's a thing), and, on the top shelf, not one but *six* Golden Toque Awards.

Big whoa.

Zoey knew all about Golden Toques. She had read about them, read interviews of chefs who had won them, seen photos and videos of them, but this was the first time she'd seen one (or six) in person. The trophies were two feet tall, shimmering gold, and shaped like the toque on Zoey's head: round on the bottom, puffy on top. They were glorious, and Zoey was on holy ground. She thought she heard angels singing and wondered if she should remove her boots. *This must be how Moses felt on Mount Sinai.*

"Dal, come here, you gotta see this."

"*Hiiii-YAH!*" At the other side of the foyer, Dallin

and the Terracotta Warrior were engaged in a no-contact, kung fu death match. He called a time-out and meandered over to the trophy case, one hand scratching his sweaty armpit.

Zoey pointed at the six trophies. "Look."

Dallin looked. And waited. "Are they gonna do something, or . . . ?"

"What? No. They're Golden Toques."

Blank look.

"Remember Royston Basil Boarhead?"

"Who?"

"The food critic? *Golden Gate Magazine*? The most powerful man in gastronomic journalism?"

"Wait, is he that dude with the eyeball in the middle of his forehead?"

"What? No. Dal, we spent like five minutes talking about him?"

"When?"

"On the cable car."

"Oh, the dork with the mustache? What about him?"

"Every July," Zoey said, "Royston Basil Boarhead and his colleagues at *Golden Gate Magazine* dine at the hottest restaurants in San Francisco. Then they nominate three candidates for a cook-off. In one day, Royston Basil Boarhead eats at each of the three candidates' restaurants. One for lunch. One for an early dinner. One for a late dinner. Then he spends the night in his home study, listening to depressing classical music and reflecting on his experience at each restaurant. Come morning, he declares one of the three restaurants the best in San Francisco and awards the head chef the Golden Toque. It's the most prestigious cooking award in the world."

"I thought Michelin stars was."

"Ah, but every year hundreds of chefs get Michelin stars. Only *one* chef gets a Golden Toque."

"What about restaurants outside of San Francisco?"

"Irrelevant. San Francisco is the Paris, France, of postmodern gastronomy."

"I thought New York was."

"Ah, but Royston Basil Boarhead is not in New York, is he?"

Dallin rubbed his hands through his hair, sending a pall of dust into the air. "So this Boarhead guy must be like the best chef in the world."

"Well, no. Most food critics aren't chefs."

"So what qualifies him to say who the best chef is?"

"Because people value his opinions."

"Why? He's not even a chef."

Zoey was starting to feel like Martha Stewart explaining nineteenth-century French table settings to that kid from *The Jungle Book*. "Trust me, Dal. He knows what he's talking about."

One of the massive red doors opened. A woman stepped out, dressed in a shimmering black tunic suit called a *zhongshan*. "Reservation?"

Zoey bowed because that's what you're supposed to do when you meet a Chinese person, right? "We're not here to eat. I'm Zoey Kate, culinary prodigy, gourmet innovator, child chef extraordinaire. And this is Dallin, a boy."

Dallin punched his right fist into his left palm and bowed. "We come in peace."

The hostess rolled her eyes.

"I'm opening a restaurant across the street. I thought

I'd pop in and meet the neighbors. Sorry I didn't bring brownies."

The hostess's almond eyes scanned Zoey up and down. "What kind of restaurant?"

"The greatest restaurant in San Francisco!"

"Who is head chef?"

"*Moi.*"

"Where did you train?"

"In my house."

"Whose recipes do you use?"

Zoey snickered. "Recipes. Right."

Slivers of light flickered across the hostess's angular face. "And your restaurant is across the street, you say?"

"Yep. Right across."

The hostess pressed her finger against a Bluetooth device fastened to her ear. She muttered something in Mandarin. She listened, nodding—was the person on the other end of the call listening to their conversation?—then said, "*Shi de.*" Whatever that meant.

The hostess bowed to Zoey and Dallin. "Chef Kung Pao will see you now."

Scallop Dumplings

Most professional kitchens are noisy, messy, chaotic places. Lots of shouting. Lots of cursing. Lots of cooks bumping into each other, leading to more shouting and more cursing. Mohawks, tattoos, and strange piercings are as commonplace as paring knives and mandolins.

But New Shanghai's kitchen was different. Every appliance and surface was spotless, including the linoleum floor. The cooks—all men—were clean-shaven, including their heads. No tattoos. No piercings. No shouting. They worked with their heads down, their eyes forward, their mouths shut. They seemed more like Shaolin monks than cooks.

The cooks wore matching double-breasted jackets, as red as China's flag. Except for one cook. His jacket was black. He wore a toque too. Also black. A braided ponytail hung the length of his broad back, tied at the bottom with bamboo twine and a rat skull. The top half of his left ear was missing. The bottom half was shriveled like rotten lettuce. He was hunched over his workstation, kneading dough with both hands.

"Is that him?" Dallin said.

"That's him," Zoey said.

Chef Pao finished the dough, wiped his hands on his apron, and looked at Zoey. His right eye was jade green. His left eye was pale and glossy like squid meat. His gaze was hard and cold like crab shells. With a wave of his hand, he beckoned Zoey—and only Zoey—to his workstation.

Zoey perked up like a cat spotting a fat mouse. "Sweet Dijon mustard, he's gonna let me watch him cook! Maybe he'll teach me some of his tricks."

"Mm," Dallin said, "I love Twix."

"Not Twix. Tricks."

"I know. I'm just saying I love Twix."

"Peanut butter or caramel?"

"Peanut butter."

"Nice."

They bumped fists.

Dallin said, "What am I supposed to do?"

"Coming through." A server popped into the kitchen, holding a stack of dirty plates and an empty bottle of Shaoxing. The area by the two-way door was narrow, so the server had to walk sideways to get past Zoey and Dallin.

"I guess you can't stand here." Zoey surveyed the kitchen, looking for an out-of-the-way spot. In one corner, three saltwater tanks sat upon wood shipping crates. Each tank was the size of those aquariums you see in doctors' and dentists' offices. One tank held mollusks. Another, crustaceans. Another, eels.

"Wait over there."

"Hey, if a kung fu fight breaks out and I roundhouse-kick

a guy into the eel tank, will the eels fry the skin off his bones?"

"Since when do you know kung fu?"

"Since I became one with the feng shui of the universe." Dallin wiggled his lips and nose in an attempt to scratch an itch on his face without using his hands. "It'd fry the skin off his bones, right?"

"Sorry, Dal. Those eels aren't electric."

"I'll warm up just in case." Dallin jogged over to the saltwater tanks and commenced a routine of knee lifts and toe touches.

Zoey scurried over to Chef Pao's workstation. Chef Pao was short, broad, and husky. He smelled like seaweed and tobacco. Zoey wondered how a man who made such pleasing food could smell so foul.

His workstation had a wooden prep board, rollers, a canister of utensils, and a rack of spices, herbs, sugars, and oils. The dough was in a big lump in a bamboo bowl. The filling sat in a pan on a two-burner stove.

Chef Pao said, "You know how cook dumpling, yes?"

"Of course."

Chef Pao clasped his hands behind his back. "You cook dumpling. If good, I serve to customer. If no good, I no serve. You cook good, yes?"

"If by 'good' you mean 'awesome,' then yes."

Chef Pao flashed a contemptuous look, like she had insulted his mother or something. "You cook good dumpling."

He lumbered away, shouldering through the two-way door into the dining parlor.

Zoey couldn't believe her luck. She had come here with

the simple hope of shaking Chef Pao's hand and taking a selfie. And now she was about to cook for him! Adrenaline pumping through her veins, Zoey gave the filling a quick stir-toss, then tried a bite: shrimp, egg whites, cilantro, garlic, soy sauce, rice vinegar, cornstarch. Not bad. Not spectacular either. It needed . . .

Dallin was doing jumping jacks. Zoey beckoned him with a nod. He came bouncing over like a dutiful puppy.

Zoey said, "Mollusks tank. Twelve scallops. Chop-chop."

"On it." Dallin hustled over to the fish tanks, peered inside, then hustled back to Zoey. "What's a scallop?"

"An edible bivalve mollusk."

Blank stare.

"Looks like the shells you'd find on a beach."

"Right." Dallin hastened back to the fish tanks.

Zoey prodded and tasted the dough. The texture was great. The flavor was great. But the color was McDonald's-bathroom-wallpaper beige. Yuck city.

She scanned her workstation. *Soy sauce . . . eel oil . . . oranges . . . mushrooms . . . Ah! Beets.*

Zoey took a plump beet, chopped it up, and stirred it into the dough. Before long, the dough was as pretty and pink as flowers on a peach tree.

Dallin arrived at Zoey's station with a dripping bucket of . . .

"Clams? Dal, I said scallops."

"You said like shells at the beach."

"Not the *ugly* shells at the beach. The pretty shells."

"Right." Dallin hurried back to the fish tanks.

To the shrimp filling, Zoey added ginger, sesame oil, black pepper, and a pinch of brown sugar.

Stirring the mix, she spotted a shrimp with the black vein—aka the "poop chute"—still attached. *Tsk, tsk. A chef of Chef Pao's stature should know better.* Zoey scooped out the shrimp and carved out the poop chute. All clean, she dropped the shrimp into the pan.

Dallin returned with a bucket of . . .

"Dude, you brought clams again!"

"You said bring the pretty shells."

"Those aren't pretty."

With the knuckle of his thumb, Dallin rubbed his forehead. "That one on top has yellow on it. Yellow's pretty, right?"

Inside the bucket, a red claw emerged from beneath the heap of clams.

"Dal, is that a—?"

"Rescue crab."

"That's not a thing."

Dallin looked desperate. "It was looking right at me, tapping the glass, begging for its life. I saw tears in its eyes, Z. Tears!"

"It was underwater."

"Might've been bubbles."

Zoey snatched the bucket from Dallin's hands. "I have to do everything myself around here."

She legged it to the fish tanks. Dallin followed. She emptied the bucket. She plunged her arm into the frigid salt water. Two at a time, she fished out scallops until her bucket was full.

Watching from behind, Dallin said, "Those look the same as the ones I picked."

"Is that so?" Setting down her bucket, Zoey reached into the tank and pulled out a clam. Hoisting the clam upon the thumb, index, and ring fingers of her left hand, she tapped the top shell with the middle finger of her right hand. In response, a plump orange muscle, four inches long, slithered out from the crack between the top and bottom shells.

Dallin took a step back. "That's one big tongue."

"It's a foot, actually. Clams don't have tongues. Watch this." Zoey transferred the clam from her fingertips to her palm. The foot "licked" her wrist, then pushed off her wrist, flipped into the air, and landed in the saltwater tank with barely a splash, like an Olympic diver, only much, much grosser.

"That," Zoey said, "is the difference between a clam and a scallop."

Dallin looked icked out and disturbed—like the time he caught his mom and her boyfriend smooching in the janitor's closet after parent-teacher conferences. "So when you said 'the pretty shells,' you meant those without pole-vaulting alien tongue-foots?"

"Precisely."

Back at her workstation, Zoey held a scallop in one hand, round side down, flat side up. With her other hand, she inserted the blade of a butter knife between the two shells. She turned the knife like a key in a lock. The shell's hinge cracked in half. She pried off the top shell and tossed it aside. From the bottom shell, she scraped and peeled away the goo and guts until all that remained was an off-white orb of tender meat ready for cooking.

After doing the same to the rest of the scallops, she added the nuggets to the pan. They sizzled and smoked and smelled like a day at the beach.

Dallin, meanwhile, had resumed his *just-in-case-kung-fu-happens* workout. This time, it was push-ups.

Zoey ripped off a chunk of dough, rolled it into the shape of a cucumber, and diced it into eight pieces. (Eight is a lucky number in China. Nice touch, right?) With a flat palm, she smashed the slices into discs the size of snicker-doodles. Using a small Asian-style roller, she flattened each disc until the center was as thick as a buttermilk pancake and the edges were as thin as a French crêpe.

After a quick stir-toss, she plucked out a scallop and popped it into her mouth.

Oh yeah. It's ready.

She scooped a glob of shrimp-and-scallop filling onto the disc of dough. She folded the dough in half like a taco, pressing the edges together to seal it up like an empanada. She severed, then sealed, the bottom left and right corners. Now the dumpling was a fan shape, like a scallop shell. With a butter knife, she etched long vertical ridges into the top of the dumpling. Soon the top resembled a scallop shell's ribbed surface. She brushed the surface with melted butter. For the final touch, she sprinkled on black and white sesame seeds to look like bits of sand from the ocean floor. Lastly, she placed the dumpling in the bamboo steamer.

One at a time, Zoey crafted seven more scallop dump-lings and put them in the steamer too. By the time she added the eighth dumpling to the steamer, the first dumpling was ready for consumption.

Zoey's nostrils flickered. *Seaweed. Tobacco. Pao's back.*

Chef Pao arrived at Zoey's workstation. He drew a pair of golden chopsticks from his jacket pocket, and clacked the tips together.

Zoey set the dumpling on a plate and served it to Chef Pao. "*Bon appétit.* Or should I say, *màn yòng?*"

Chef Pao looked impressed. "You speak Chinese?"

"No," Zoey said, "but I know how to say '*bon appétit*' in fifty-two languages."

Impressed look: gone. Chef Pao seized the dumpling with his chopsticks, raised it to his chin. He smelled it. He popped it into his mouth. He chewed. His expression was blank. No sign of approval or disapproval, nirvana or disgust. No "This tastes amazing" or "With every bite I wish for death."

I bet he's good at poker.

Chef Pao pointed his chopsticks at a door at the back of the kitchen. "You two. Come."

Chinese Takeout

The alley behind New Shanghai smelled like a clogged garbage disposal. It was as narrow as the cereal aisle at Walmart and as long as the Great Wall of China. Felt like it, at least. The alley walls were so tall they blocked out all sunlight, making the warm afternoon feel like a chilly evening.

Chef Pao closed the back door. He turned to face Zoey and Dallin, and tugged on his shriveled ear, like it wasn't attached right and needed adjusting.

Zoey said, "Um, why'd you bring us out here?"

Chef Pao did not answer. With his hands behind his back, he stepped toward the two youths. His breathing was slow and measured like that of a dragon. His jade eye glowed with menace. (His other eye was just gross.) "Property across street no available."

Zoey said, "But the sign in the window says it's for rent."

Chef Pao continued forward. "No. You go to different street. Different city. Far away."

Dallin grabbed Zoey's wrist. It was a protective gesture, Dallin's way of saying, "If things get crazy, I got your back."

Zoey took a step back. Broken glass crackled beneath her boots. "You can't tell me where to open my restaurant. You don't own San Francisco."

With smooth, even steps, Chef Pao backed Zoey and Dallin deeper into the shadows of the long, damp alley. He put forth his right hand, fingers still clutching those golden chopsticks. He clacked the tips together. *Tk. Tk. Tk. Tk.* "Ah, but I *do* own San Francisco. If I say you no open restaurant, then you no open restaurant. Or else."

"Or else what?"

"Or else . . ." *Tk. Tk. Tk.* ". . . pain."

Dallin gripped Zoey's wrist. "He wants to eat us."

"No," Zoey said, "just scare us."

Chef Pao's right hand lunged forward like a striking cobra. The chopsticks clacked together, a mere inch from Zoey's nose, before pulling back again. Chef Pao could have given her nose quite a pinch. And that was the point. He could have. It was a warning.

"Good thing I stretched." Dallin went into a kung fu stance. Sort of. He stood on one leg, the other leg raised. One hand was in a fist, the other hand was above his head, fingers curled like eagle talons.

"*Hiiii-YAH!*" Dallin attempted a roundhouse kick. He only made it halfway around, so the kick went in the opposite direction of its intended target.

It was official: Dallin did *not* know kung fu.

Dallin turned to face Chef Pao again. "There's more where that came from, homeslice."

Holding the chopsticks with tips together, like he was about to dig into a bowl of crisp veggies, Chef Pao jabbed Dallin in the belly.

Dallin recoiled, hands clutching the spot where he'd been hit. "Oh, come on!"

"Hey!" Zoey said. "Watch where you're poking those— *OUCH!*"

Chef Pao had jabbed her in the stomach too. It hurt, like a poke from a sharp stick.

Dallin cried out, "Samuraiiiiiiiii-*PUNCH!*" He ran at Chef Pao, swinging his fists like a frantic gorilla.

Undaunted, Chef Pao caught Dallin's left wrist in his chopsticks. Chef Pao turned his hand, bending Dallin's whole arm, driving him to the ground. It was impressive, actually. Had Chef Pao done that to someone other than Dallin, Zoey might have applauded.

"Run, Z!" Dallin cried. "He's a ninja!"

Zoey helped Dallin to his feet. "Ninjas are Japanese."

"Whatever! Just run!"

Zoey and Dallin ran for it.

Chef Pao called after them, "You no open restaurant. I always watching. You never safe."

Still running, Zoey glanced back over her shoulder at Chef Pao. He was laughing.

Indigestion

Zoey pounded up California Street, fuming like an overheated Teflon pan. "Lousy Pao . . . thinks he owns San Francisco . . . heartless excuse for a chef . . . supposed to be a role model . . ."

Dallin was ten steps behind, rasping and staggering like a bloated zombie. "Still . . . digesting . . . two pounds . . . hoagie awesomeness . . ."

An SFMTA bus, bigger than a blue whale, screamed past, bellowing stinky black exhaust. Coughing and hacking, Zoey clamped her hands on her head to keep her toque from flying away. "Lousy bus . . . thinks it owns the air . . . heartless excuse for a motorized vehicle . . . I'll open my restaurant wherever I wanna open my restaurant . . ."

Dallin pounded his fists against his barrel chest, prompting a mighty belch. "There it is." He ran to catch up with Zoey. "Hey, can we get something to eat? I'm starving."

"I'm too furious to eat."

"Can we sit down, at least? My legs kill."

"I'm too furious to sit."

Dallin grabbed his gut. "Oop! There's a cramp."

A police siren sounded in the distance. Its shrill cry bounced off stucco high-rises and dusty windowpanes. "Why didn't I think of that?" She stopped and took out her iPhone.

Dallin caught up to her, panting like a dog after a game of fetch. "Who're you calling?"

"The cops."

"*NO!*" Dallin slapped the iPhone out of Zoey's hand. It landed on the sidewalk, screen down.

"Dude!" Zoey stooped and picked up the phone. She brushed off the screen. No cracks. *Phew.* "What is your problem?"

"Cops are a bad idea, Z."

Zoey wondered if Dallin had bumped his head on something hard when she wasn't looking. "Chef Pao has no right to tell me where I can and can't open a restaurant."

Zoey dialed 9— "Hey!"

Dallin had batted the phone out of her hands again.

"Dude! Are you *trying* to break my phone?"

"I'm *trying* to keep you out of trouble."

"Me?" Zoey picked up her phone again. Still no cracks. *Phew again.* "I'm not the one who attacked us with chopsticks. That was Chef Pao, remember? He committed assault. That means jail time. Plus, we're minors, so I'm pretty sure he'll get the electric chair."

She dialed 1—

Dallin snatched the phone from her hands.

"Give it back."

"Let me explain."

Zoey tried to snatch the phone back. Dallin was too

quick. He held the phone high above his head so she couldn't reach it.

"Dallin Caraway, if you don't give me back my phone you'll be in big, big trouble." *Eckk. I sound like my mom.*

Dallin said, "You don't watch many movies, do you?"

"I watch tons of movies."

"Not cooking movies. Real movies, with guns and car chases and stuff."

"Oh, those."

"I watch a lotta movies, Z, so I know how this works. Anytime two kids are up against a bad guy—doesn't matter if it's a Mafia boss, or a swamp monster, or, in our case, a psychotic samurai chef—"

"Samurais aren't Chi—"

"The point is, the worst thing we can do is tell an adult. I've seen it a thousand times, Z. Kids encounter a bad guy, they tell their parents, their parents call the cops, the cops show up, and then—*twist*—one of the cops *is* the bad guy."

Zoey considered this for a moment, and then . . . "Gimme that phone." She lunged at Dallin. He turned. She landed on him, piggyback-style. They wriggled and squirmed and grappled and grunted, spinning like a wobbly top, until Dallin said, "All right, here, take it."

Zoey took the phone and hopped off Dallin. They stood there, on the sidewalk, huffing and puffing like they'd swum ten laps around Alcatraz Island.

Zoey said, "Did you call Chef Pao 'homeslice'?"

Dallin averted his eyes. "Sorry you had to hear that."

"Me too." Zoey looked at her phone. During the hullabaloo, Dallin had pushed like a zillion numbers, including a few fractions, which Zoey hadn't known was possible. Zoey cleared the numbers, typed in 9-1-1, then paused.

What if Dallin is right? Not about Chef Pao turning out to be a two-faced cop; that's ludicrous. But what if telling the authorities does indeed lead to more trouble than it's worth? The cops would tell my parents, right? I mean, they have to. Valentine would freak. She'd be like, "You're never going anywhere alone ever again. And you're never opening a restaurant. And you can't be friends with Dallin anymore. And no more Chinese food."

Too much was at risk. She put the phone in her pocket. "What do we do now?"

"The only thing we can do," Dallin said. "Drive a stake through Chef Pao's heart."

"Maybe we should check out the other addresses on my list first."

"There's that too."

"Let's go."

Location, Location, Location

 First, Zoey and Dallin went to 1530 Fillmore Street and peeked through the windows. (Stained carpet. Holes in the walls. Leaky ceiling. No thank you.)

So they checked out the next property on the list, 25 W. Portal Avenue. (Shared a wall with a scream-therapy clinic. Um, no.)

So they checked out 1B Mission Street. (Occupied by squatters.)

Then Dallin said, "If I don't eat soon, I'll die." So they dipped into Little Saigon Deli to get him a chicken-and-waffle sandwich.

Then they checked out 197 Gough Street. (Below a tap-dancing studio.)

Then, since they were in the neighborhood, they ducked into Otoro Sushi to see how many avocado rolls Dallin could eat in one minute. (Thirty-two.) The manager insisted they never come back.

Next, Zoey and Dallin checked out 231 Franklin Street. (Rat infestation.)

Then 374 Broadway. (Haunted.)

Then 558 Valencia Street. (Rat infestation. And haunted. Go figure.)

Then Dallin declared a "state of emergency" in his digestive track, claiming the avocado rolls and chicken-and-waffle sandwich had united against him in full rebellion. He lay down on a bus stop bench to "sleep until the war is over."

Forty-five minutes later, Zoey and Dallin were at 331 Eddy Street, gripping the burglar bars on the windows, peering through the dusty glass, counting the bullet holes in the walls and ceiling.

Dallin said, "I count forty-two."

Zoey said, "Did you count the cluster by the stairs as one or six?"

"I missed those. Forty-eight."

Zoey turned from the burglar bars. "Finding a good property in this city is harder than I'd thought."

"I'm hungry," Dallin said.

She took out her iPhone and dialed her real estate agent. He answered after one ring.

"Happy Curry Real Estate, where you do the work and we get the commission. This is Sandesh speaking. How may I help you?"

"Hey. It's Zoey. I checked out the properties you referred me to. All losers. Go ahead and shoot me a dozen more addresses to check out."

"One moment." Zoey heard the *clack clack clack* of Sandesh's fingers typing on a keyboard. "Hmmm. A dozen may be difficult."

"Half a dozen, then."

"Hmmm. Half a dozen may be difficult."

"One, then?"

"Hmmm. One may be difficult."

Zoey's grip tightened on her phone. "Of all the properties in San Francisco, the only ones available are the ones I've already seen?"

"Hmmm." More typing. "Ah. Here's a beautiful property. Three thousand square feet. Vaulted ceilings. Ocean view. In Presidio."

"I love Presidio. How much?"

"Three million."

"I'm no mathematician, Sandesh, but I'm pretty sure that exceeds my budget."

"Hmmm." More typing. "Ah. There is a walnut farm for sale. It's in Stockton."

"I'm gonna have to fire you, aren't I?"

"Tell your friends."

Zoey ended the call. Her blood boiled like hot tomato soup. She kicked a POLICE VEHICLES ONLY sign near the curb. "I am *not* loving San Francisco right now."

Dallin had his back against the burglar bars, his arms folded, his hands in fists to prop up his biceps. "Now what?"

It was evening now. The sun was on its way out, and the fog was on its way in. The fog was a welcome sight, as far as Zoey was concerned. She wished the fog would engulf her, make her disappear, make her forget the hopelessness gnawing at her heart.

"Now," Zoey said, "we wallow. We're four blocks from the city's best Italian restaurant. It'll be crowded, but I'm tight with the owner. He'll get us a table. We'll sit down, order too much food, and eat until our emotions are numb. How's that sound?"

Dallin pumped his fist in the air. "Suh-weet."

La Cucina di Cannoli

La Cucina di Cannoli smelled like butter and garlic and olive oil and focaccia bread. Grapevines and murals of Tuscan orchards adorned the walls. Red-and-white-checkered tablecloths draped square tables. Empty wine bottles wrapped in ribbons and filled with raw farfalle pasta served as the tables' centerpieces. A selection from Verdi's *La Traviata* sang from small HD speakers in the domed ceiling.

Diners wore suits and gowns and shiny jewelry, and the low lighting made them appear more attractive than they really were. Zoey and Dallin, on the other hand, looked like they'd emerged from a homeless shelter. Their clothes were wrinkled and sooty, their faces sweaty and dirty (Dallin more so than Zoey). On a normal evening, Zoey would've never gone anywhere in this state. But right now she was too tired, too hungry, and too bummed out to care.

At the podium by the front door, a hostess greeted Zoey and Dallin with a toothy smile. Zoey didn't recognize her. *She must be new.*

The hostess opened her reservations book. "Name?"

Yep. She's new.

"Please tell Chef Cannoli that Zoey Kate is here."

The hostess moved her finger down the page, making clicking sounds with her tongue. "Hmmm. I don't see it. Perhaps you made the reservation under a different name?"

Zoey reached over the podium and closed the hostess's book. "Let me bring you up to speed. I'm Zoey Kate, culinary prodigy, gourmet innovator, child chef extraordinaire. You may call me Chef. I'm a regular here. Chef Cannoli and I go way back. He gave me my first panini press. I made the wedding cakes for his third and fourth marriages. We've been trading recipes for years. The tiramisu on your menu, that's mine."

By chance, a server rushed past carrying two plates of pecan-pesto shells and sausage. "*Ciao*, Chef Zoey. Always a pleasure."

Zoey smirked at the hostess. "See?"

The hostess flushed. "Sorry, Chef Zoey. I'll notify him now." She picked up the phone, pushed a button, and waited. "Hello, Chef, sorry to bother you, but, um, Chef Zoey is here and . . . Okay, I will. Okay, thank you." She hung up the phone. "Chef Cannoli is in his office. I'll be happy to escort you if—"

"I know the way."

Zoey led Dallin across the dining parlor. Their shabby appearances garnered a few disapproving looks from the immaculate patrons, but nothing to snivel about.

At the back of the restaurant were two doors. The door on the right, a two-way, led to the kitchen. The door on the left led to Chef Cannoli's office. Zoey gave the door on the left a brisk, one-knuckle *tap-tap*, then opened it and walked in, bringing Dallin with her.

Chef Cannoli rose from a chair behind the old wooden table that served as his desk. "*Ciao*, Chef Zoey, what pleasant surprise is this."

The chef wore a collared shirt the color of Parmesan, unbuttoned to his sternum, a fancy gold watch too big for his skinny wrist, espresso slacks with creases so sharp they could cut through Fiore Sardo, and Borgioli designer shoes. His white hair, wavy on the sides, thin on top, looked disheveled and whippy, like he'd been pulling on it all day.

Zoey wondered why he wasn't wearing his chef whites. *Maybe he's saving his energy for the weekend. Everyone knows the best chefs work weekends.*

Chef Cannoli reached into an umbrella stand next to the desk and withdrew a long black cane. At the top of the cane perched a gold lion's head, four inches tall, its jaws open in a silent roar. Leaning on his cane, Chef Cannoli hobbled around his desk to greet Zoey.

"That's new," Zoey said of the cane.

"Is nothing, this," Chef Cannoli said, smiling, "I don't know why I got old. What thing was I thinking?"

Zoey and Chef Cannoli hugged. Chef Cannoli kissed her on the cheek as was the greeting custom in his native Tuscany. Zoey liked this custom very much.

"Chef Cannoli, this is Dallin."

"*Un piacere.*" Chef Cannoli leaned forward to kiss Dallin's cheek.

Dallin raised his arms in front of his face. "This ain't Europe, dude. Keep your lips to yourself."

Chef Cannoli clicked his tongue against the roof of his

mouth. *"Americano tipico."* He placed his liver-spotted left hand under Zoey's chin. *"Bambina,* when I look at your pretty face I see only the worry and the sadness. What thing to you is happened?"

"Rough day," Zoey said.

"Poor *bambina."* Chef Cannoli pointed his cane at two chairs in front of his desk. "Please, have a place to sit. I give to you something *delizioso* for eat. A good meal lifts the heavy soul, no?"

"Merci and *grazie,"* Zoey said as she and Dallin took their seats.

Chef Cannoli pressed a button on a small intercom on his desk. Static. "Panzanella?"

A woman's voice answered: *"Sì,* Chef?"

"Tre spaghetti e polpette, per favore."

"Sì, Chef."

As Chef Cannoli limped back to his side of the desk, Zoey admired the many awards on his walls. There were framed certificates of achievement from the Julia Child Foundation, the Culinary Institute of America, the Academia Barilla of Parma, and the Italian American Heritage Foundation. A wall-mounted shelf held well-polished plaques and trophies, most notably a James Beard Award and two Michelin stars. Above that shelf was another shelf: a smaller shelf, square, with nothing on it.

I wonder what that's for.

Two bookshelves stood against a wall. One bookshelf held fun books with titles like *1,001 Uses for Fettuccine, 1521: The Year Michelangelo Made Asiago Cool Again,* and *Eat Carbs, Stay Thin: The Joy of Italian Cooking.* The other bookshelves held boring books like *The Small*

Business Owner's Guide to Taxes & Fines, *Red Tape: Everything You Must Know About Employee Health & Safety*, and *She's Having A Baby: How Maternity Leave Affects Your Bottom Line*.

The fun books were in mint condition. The spines looked crisp and smooth. No wrinkles. Chef Cannoli hadn't read or even touched them. The boring books were worn-out, beat-up, and dog-eared, like he'd read them daily for decades. *Poor guy.*

Chef Cannoli settled into his chair and laid the cane on his lap. "Please pardon the disorder." He panned his hand over untidy stacks of invoices, receipts, proofs of purchase, credit card bills, and tax documents on his desk. "I have much busy, but I make tidy of this."

He commenced gathering up the papers and transferring them into desk drawers and baskets on a nearby shelf. Zoey felt useless, sitting there watching him tidy up by himself. But she didn't pitch in either. Those papers contained business-sensitive information, and Zoey wanted to respect his privacy.

While Chef Cannoli tidied up, Dallin leaned over to Zoey and whispered, "Hey, ask him about the Olive Garden name thing."

Zoey whispered back, "How would he know? He doesn't work for Olive Garden."

"It's his people. They talk. He'll know."

Chef Cannoli finished tidying his desk. "So, *bambina*, what did happen to make to you a, how did you say, rough day?"

Zoey folded her arms on the tabletop. "Me and Dallin were in Chinatown. We ran into Chef Pao and—"

Chef Cannoli pounded his fist on the desk. "Pao—I curse the name! He always is winning the Golden Toque, six years in rows like he is the god of cooking. *Es un sacrilegio!* I am come to worry that *Golden Gate Magazine* has no more the taste for the fine cooking."

"I hope not," Zoey said, "otherwise I'll never win one."

Dallin leaned forward, planted his elbows on his knees, and looked Chef Cannoli in the eyes. "About the Olive Garden . . ."

A server came into the room. Panzanella, presumably. Her silky black hair hung past her waist and shimmered like caviar, and her ornate gold earrings jangled like Christmas tree ornaments. She carried a big, round serving tray, from which she served them three heaping plates of spaghetti and meatballs, a basket of steaming garlic Parmesan rolls, and three glasses of iced pomegranate juice. Next to each plate she placed a maroon silverware roll-up. *"Buon appetito,"* she said with a pretty smile. She strode out of the room, her long hair swaying like a silk cape.

Being in the company of an Italian chef, Zoey decided to eat her spaghetti the Italian way. She unwrapped her silverware and tucked the napkin into the neck of her jacket. She took the fork in her right hand, the spoon in her left. She held the spoon bowl-down at a forty-five-degree angle. With her fork, she speared a clump of saucy noodles. She planted the fork's teeth in the bowl of the spoon. She rotated the fork clockwise until the noodles swaddled the fork. Leaning forward, she positioned her head over her plate and inserted the bundle of noodles into her mouth. "Best spaghetti in San Francisco," she said between chews.

Chef Cannoli placed a hand over his heart and bowed his head.

Dallin stabbed his fork into a meatball the size of a tennis ball and proceeded to cram the greasy sphere into his mouth. It took some finagling, but he made it fit.

"For what reason you were in Chinatown?" Chef Cannoli asked, slicing his fork through the center of a chunky meatball.

Zoey tore a hot, buttery roll in half. "Checking out real estate. I'm starting a restaurant."

Chef Cannoli dropped his saucy fork. His upper body went as rigid as dried fettuccini. "Are you sure you want to do that?"

"Super sure."

"But you are a chef, *bambina*. You should not be running a *ristorante*. You should be cooking."

"Oh, I'll do all the cooking. I'm the only chef."

Chef Cannoli tittered and shook his head. "That is how I had the thoughts when I started La Cucina. Then I had it to learn how things really happen. Running a *ristorante* is so much of the work. Most of the work is not for the cooking. Is for the other things. To keep it clean the men's restroom is part-time job. Do you know what means the Code Brown?"

Zoey and Dallin shook their heads.

"You will," Chef Cannoli said. "I recommend you to have a big toilet brush and a big mop."

"Gross," Dallin said.

"In beginning, I did all from solo—the cooking, the service, the cleaning, the labor of office, *e tutto*. I work for twenty hours of day, seven days of week. Many nights I have the feeling so exhausted that I sleep on the kitchen floor."

Zoey's eyes lit up like veal flambé. "Sounds awesome."

"Yes, but . . ." Chef Cannoli rubbed a thumb across the gray stubble on his chin. ". . . but in time it becomes . . . *troppo* . . . what is word?"

"Super awesome?"

"Too much. Yes, *troppo*, too much. So I hire sous chef to assist me in the cooking. It takes three months for to train the sous chef. Then one sous chef no is enough, so I hire a second sous chef. Then the IRS comes to say I owe to the government more taxes."

Zoey knew all about taxes. Taxes were why she had to pay a buck-oh-eight for a ninety-nine-cent chocolate bar. The extra nine cents went to the government to pay for wars and the president's vacations. But she didn't understand why an IRS (whatever that was, probably a robot) had come around demanding he pay more. "They made you pay the same taxes twice?"

Chef Cannoli looked puzzled. (Dallin kept eating. He had tuned them out.) Chef Cannoli said, "What you mean to say, twice?"

"You know, you buy a can opener, you pay the tax, and that's it. You're done. Why'd you have to pay again?"

Chef Cannoli chuckled in a way that made Zoey feel young and naïve. "You speak of the sales tax. The government came to collect from me the *income tax*."

"Income?" Zoey said. "As in all-the-money-I-make?"

Cannoli frowned. "Yes."

"Hold on. Whoa. You're telling me . . ." Zoey tried

(and failed) to soften the edge in her voice. ". . . the government makes us pay taxes on every dollar we spend *and earn?*"

"The more of the money we make, the more is for the government to take."

"In Italy or America?"

"Both."

Zoey thought about all the money she'd made from four years of covert Lunch Rush ops.

Uh-oh. Was I supposed to pay taxes on that? Nah, of course not. I'm a kid. Kids don't pay income tax, right? I don't even know how much money I've made. How am I supposed to pay taxes if I don't know how much money I made? It's not like I can travel back in time. What if the government decides I owe them money and they dispatch an IRS (probably stands for Insidious Robot Soldier) to hunt me down and laser-blast me?

No, of course not. I'm being ridiculous. The government doesn't send robots to kill people. They got drones for that.

(Note to self: make arrangements for one or two false identities, just in case.)

The room was, like, a zillion degrees now. Zoey picked up her cold pomegranate juice. "How much does the government take, exactly?" She took a big, long drink.

"If you have much of the success, like me, then you pay . . ." Chef Cannoli's frown became even frownier. "Half."

Zoey did a spit-take. Red juice sprayed Chef Cannoli's face and his shirt and his spaghetti and meatballs and his table/desk.

"Nice," Dallin said without looking up from his plate.

"So sorry," Zoey said.

Chef Cannoli chuckled the way a grandpa does when his grandkids get butterscotch pudding all over their faces. "Is okay. That was my first reaction too."

Chef Cannoli used his maroon cloth napkin to wipe off his face and shirt. "So the IRS say I have to pay to them the incomes taxes. I pass weeks for dig up of the receipts and the orders and the papers from the bank. My restaurant it gets many and many the customers and my two cooks no can to handle it, so I forced to hire a three chef.

"Then the first chef, he slips on wet floor and breaks himself the ankle. He no more can cook. Lawyer man tells me I have to pay because of the fall in my restaurant. I am the *responsabilità*. I say to the lawyer man, 'I no have it the insurance.' He says, 'Then you have the problem.'

"I have to pay money to the hospital for to fix the first chef ankle. I have to hire a four chef to do the work of the first chef. First chef tells me, 'My ankle will be better, I will come back to cook the food,' but he no come back. *Bugiardo*.

"Now I am to pass all of the day and all of the night at desk, buying the insurance, paying the taxes, making the paperwork. One day, I look around. I say, 'What did happen?' I have twelve cooks in my kitchen. I am too much busy to cook. Today I no wear myself the chef whites because I no more have time for the cooking."

Zoey gasped. "That's horrible."

"*Sì*, is very, very horrible. But . . ." Chef Cannoli patted Zoey's arm. ". . . I am sure that you figure out. *Mi scusi*, *per favore*, I must verify if the cash register has enough of the receipt paper. Enjoy you the spaghetti. Remain as much long as you have desire."

Chef Cannoli stood and, leaning on his cane, tottered around the table/desk. He kissed Zoey on the cheek, smiled at Dallin (who had his hands up, karate-chop-style), and exited the room.

Dallin went back to chowing down. Zoey did not. She felt like she had an anvil in her stomach. And the anvil was covered in spikes. And the spikes were impaling tiny cuddly teddy bears. And the teddy bears were reading *The Communist Manifesto* and saying "That's a good point" a lot.

She sank in her chair, unable to eat. "Do you think Chef Cannoli is right?"

"No idea." Dallin licked a streak of marinara sauce off the back of his hand. "I couldn't understand a word that dude said. Except for the Code Brown thing. That I got."

Zoey pushed away her plate, feeling sicker by the second.

Dallin raised his fork. "Mind if I . . . ?"

"Fine."

Dallin scooped Zoey's spaghetti onto his plate. "What did Cana-olives say that's got you so depressed?"

"It's Cannoli."

"What'd I say?"

"You said 'Cana-olives.'"

"Sounds the same," Dallin said.

Zoey yanked the napkin from her collar and plonked it on the table. "He said owning a restaurant is all bills and taxes and messy bathrooms and sitting at a desk and not cooking. Do you think he's right?"

Dallin nibbled the char off a meatball. "Dunno, Z. I've never owned a restaurant."

Zoey looked at the bookshelves: the untouched fun books and well-used boring books. "Maybe he is right. I mean, I've been up since six a.m., I've worked all day trying to find a stupid property to rent, without success, mind you, and I haven't done a minute of cooking. I can't even think of a cool restaurant name. Maybe Chef Cannoli did me a favor. Maybe I need to jump ship. Get out before it's too late."

This time Dallin did the spit-take. "You're not gonna open a restaurant now?"

"I'm not giving up cooking. But maybe I'd be better off, I don't know, working as a line cook or something, in someone else's restaurant."

Dallin glared with suspicion. "Who are you and what have you done with Zoey Kate?"

"Finish up," Zoey said. "I wanna go home."

The Spirit of San Francisco

Zoey and Dallin stood on the corner of California and Hyde, waiting for a cable car. It was night. The wind blew, cold and wet like a sea urchin. Headlights, streetlights, and traffic lights glowed in the crawling fog like UFOs. Zoey tucked her hands in her skirt pockets to shield them from the biting cold.

Unaffected by the cold, Dallin drummed his fingers on his round belly like it was a *djembe*. "You could get a food truck."

"I'm not a barbarian," Zoey said.

"People like food trucks."

"Out of the question."

Dallin burped, then flinched at how bad it smelled. "It's too bad your Italian friend didn't offer us dessert. I could go Godzilla on a hot-fudge sundae right about now."

"Mmmm." Zoey tilted her head to one side, savoring the thought. "With glazed maraschino cherries."

"And crushed-up graham crackers."

"And melted marshmallows."

A cable car emerged from the fog like a torpedo in slow

motion. Its maroon shutters and silver spindles glimmered in the streetlights. Riders sat on an open deck, chatting, laughing, and sipping hot chocolates. On the trolley's flat front, flowing gold letters spelled the words:

The Spirit of San Francisco

Dallin pulled his arms into his shirt, giving his forearms and hands some relief from the cold. "Hey, do you think the cable car sells hot chocolate?"

"Nah." Zoey blew on her fingers. "Those folks must've bought them before boarding."

"Bummer," Dallin said. "I'd pay five bucks for a hot chocolate right now."

Something curious happened then. The cable car *changed*. Its colors, maroon and silver, transformed into bold shades of red, black, and gold. Inside the car, men and women sat at square tables draped in white linen. They dined on filet mignon, prosciutto-wrapped asparagus, and garlic croissants stuffed with Brie cheese. And there was Zoey, in an open-view kitchen nook, dressed in a red, black, and gold jacket and toque, ladling strawberry sauce over a freshly baked cheesecake. On the front of the car, the gold letters rearranged themselves into a new name. One word. Simple. Beautiful.

Zoeylicious

The name sank into Zoey's psyche like butter on a hot croissant. Mesmerized, she whispered the name. "Zoeylicious." It tasted sweeter than blueberry crêpes.

Spellbound, Zoey waved her hand to the side until it hit Dallin's arm. "Hey, Dal, you seeing what I'm seeing?"

"A homeless guy screaming at a parking meter?"

"No, I mean the— Wait. What?"

Dallin pointed across the street. A man in tattered clothes was wringing a parking meter's neck, so to speak. "They're onto us, Claire! They know about St. Louis— the money, the fire, the mannequin, everything! We'll burn for this, Claire! *BUUUUURN!*" The man ran away, weeping.

"Not that." Zoey pressed her hand against Dallin's cheek, redirecting his gaze to the cable car. "That."

Dallin made an *either-you're-nuts-or-I'm-missing-something-here* face. (If you've ever showed a friend your "groundbreaking" invisible stamps collection, you've seen it.) "Is something behind the cable car, or . . . ?"

"Not *behind* the cable car. It *is* the cable car."

"What is the cable car?"

"It's Zoeylicious!"

"Zoey-what-now?"

Zoey didn't know if she was dreaming or hallucinating or having an out-of-body experience or what. But there it was. Not a cable car; those are bound to a fixed route. But a trolley. With wheels and a dining parlor and kitchen nook. And heaters, presumably. The mobility and convenience of a food truck with the comfort and trappings of a five-star restaurant. The ultimate fine-dining experience. It was perfect. It was glorious. It was . . .

My restaurant.

Adrenaline shot through Zoey's muscles like electricity. She threw her arms around Dallin's broad shoulders and squeezed him like he was a giant lemon. "You, Dallin Caraway, are a genius."

Dallin was a tackler, not a hugger, so he didn't respond well to hugging. His entire body went rigid, his cold cheeks turned redder than enchilada sauce, and his heart stopped pumping blood. Zoey released him so he wouldn't die.

"Thanks." Dallin thumped his fist on his chest, jump-starting the blood flow. "Uh, why am I a genius?"

"A restaurant on a trolley. It's brilliant and classy and timeless, and you led me right to it."

"I did?"

"You did!"

Dallin brightened. "I did!"

Zoey threw her hands in the air like she just didn't care. She jumped and clicked her heels and shrieked with delight. Dallin whipped off his shirt, swung it above his head like a lasso, and galloped in circles like a cowboy.

Zoey stopped. "Dude, what're you doing?"

Dallin stopped too. His shirt landed on his head. "Celebrating."

"This isn't Niners stadium. Put your shirt back on."

"Right." Dallin put his shirt back on. "Whoo, that was cold."

The cable car stopped. No passengers got off, and no passengers got on.

Dallin, who always let Zoey board first, said, "We doing this or not?"

"Not," Zoey said. "We got work to do."

She motioned to the conductor to keep on moving. The cable car glided down Hyde Street and disappeared into the fog.

"Do you feel that, Dal?"

"Doubt it."

"It's purpose. As in 'this is my purpose in life.' This is what God sent me to do. To share my food with the world. To make people happy. To give friends and families a reason to sit down together, put away their phones, forget about their worries, and live for an hour. All that stuff Chef Cannoli was talking about: Code Browns, taxes, injuries, lawyers, insurance—it's in the weeds. What matters is the people. I will not rest until every man, woman, and child (minus those with severe allergies and enzyme intolerances) partakes of the work of my hands, and experiences a little bit of gastronomic heaven."

Dallin picked a piece of cheddar out of his nose. "So where do we get a trolley?"

Hog Vomit Junkyard

 Zoey peered through the gaps in a tall barbed-wire fence at the hugest junkyard she'd ever seen. (Not that she had a lot of experience with junkyards, but still . . .) The lot was the size of Giants stadium. Busted automobiles, expired appliances, and mountains of scrap metal formed a metropolis of rot and ruin. All that was missing was a lovable robot named WALL-E.

"It smells worse than it looks," she said, a bitter metallic odor filling her nostrils.

Dallin stood beside her. In his dirty, tattered clothes and the gloom of a cold, foggy night, he looked like a zombie. (Minus the *I-wanna-eat-your-brains* stuff.) "Does he work here or live here?"

"Both, I think," Zoey said.

"It doesn't look safe."

"Of course it's not safe. That's why you're here, Dal, to protect us."

Dallin tapped his fingertips on a porcelain toilet seat bolted to a slab of sheet metal bolted to a wood pole. "Is this the . . . ?"

"Must be." Zoey rapped the toilet seat against the sheet metal like it was a door knocker. The metallic CLAAAAAAAANG ricocheted through the junkyard like a clumsy bullet. A murder of crows sprang from the broken windows of an upside-down ambulance, cawing like banshees, wings flapping hard and fast.

They waited.

Dallin said, "Do you think he heard it?"

From the greasy bowels of the junkyard, an engine roared to life.

"Yep," Zoey said, "he heard it."

A plume of dust spun upward from behind a wall of oil drums and trash cubes, accompanied by the sound of rubber tires on dirt and gravel.

The engine's growl grew louder and louder as the spiral of dust raced toward Zoey and Dallin like a hungry tornado. A black Harley-Davidson screamed into view. Astride the motorcycle sat Knuckles Andwich, his bald head and tattooed arms glinting in the moonlight.

Knuckles rode to the fence, skidded to a stop, and planted both feet on the ground. The Harley's chrome engine purred like a panther enjoying a foot massage. (If that doesn't win me a Pulitzer, nothing will.)

Knuckles raised his hands above his head. "I didn't know they was stolen, officers! If I had, I woulda never hid 'em in a place you'll never find, at a location I can't recall. Swear on the Bible!"

"Knuckles, it's me, Chef Zoey."

Knuckles reached into a gear bag mounted on the rear fender. He took out a flashlight, aimed the beam at his visitors. "Chef Zoey?"

"Hey. This is my friend Dallin."

Dallin put his arms through his sleeves like normal. Then he fake-yawned, fake-stretching his arms to show off his biceps. "Yeah, I'm getting a tattoo soon. Something with skulls and blood on it. My mom says I'm too young to get a tattoo, but I'm getting one anyway. I'm a rebel. People don't wanna mess with me."

Knuckles dismounted, leaning the Harley on its kick-stand. He strode to the gate, flashlight fixed on the two youths. "It's eleven o'clock. What're ya kids doin' out 'ere? Why aren't ya at home? Where're yer parents?"

Zoey held up a hand to shield the light from her eyes. "My parents are jazz musicians. In my house, eleven o'clock isn't late."

Dallin said, "My mom has a loose parenting style."

Knuckles lowered the flashlight. "Why'd ya come?"

"I need to procure a trolley and turn it into a restaurant," Zoey said. "You and your gang are always collecting and restoring old vehicles and stuff. Can you help me out?"

"Sorry, kiddo. That kinda job'd take some serious cabbage."

"Is fifty grand serious enough?"

Knuckles nearly dropped his flashlight. "Ya got fifty g's?"

"I need to keep some for ingredients, but yeah."

Knuckles ran his oil-stained fingers through his bushy black beard. "Come on in. I got sumthin' t' show ya."

Trolley, Trolley, Trolley

In a well-lit corner of the junkyard, behind a heaping wall of hubcaps and old mattresses, Zoey and Dallin stood shoulder to elbow gawking at three dilapidated trolleys. The trolleys were linked together like train cars. Their tires were flat, their windows broken, their paint faded and peeling.

"They're pieces of junk," Dallin said.

"They just need a little TLC," Zoey said.

"More like CPR," Dallin said.

Knuckles leaned his Harley on its kickstand. "They're old-school, all right. Built in the eighteen hundreds. Been here at Hog Vomit longer than I 'ave. I got no use for 'em, so, if ya want 'em, I'll give ya three fer the price o' one."

"Let's have a look, shall we?" Zoey climbed aboard the first trolley. The cabin was long and empty, the carpet threadbare, the old light fixtures draped in cobwebs.

"*Guh,*" Dallin said, stepping aboard. "Smells like the men's bathroom at Levi's Stadium."

Knuckles boarded next. "Smells fine t' me. Of course,

I used t' *live* in the men's bathroom at Levi's Stadium, so, yeah, that was a rough summer."

"It's perfect!" Zoey pranced through the cabin, giddier than a monkey at a banana farm. "The walk-in will go here . . . the conventional ovens here and here and here . . . the brick oven here . . . the Dutch oven there . . . the cocoa grinder there . . . the fire pit over—"

"Fire pit?" Knuckles said.

"How else am I supposed to make s'mores? Now, where to put my anvil?"

At the front end of the cabin, Dallin opened a narrow door leading to the driver's box. "Steering wheel's gone," he announced. "What are all these levers for?"

Knuckles was leaning against a wall, cleaning his fingernails with the blade of a pocketknife. "The levers *are* the steerin' wheel, kiddo, 'n the gas, 'n the brake. Like I said, old-school."

Dallin said, "Looks hard to drive."

Knuckles said, "It *is* hard t' drive."

Zoey said to Knuckles. "Can you drive it?"

Knuckles said, "I reckon I could."

Zoey said, "That settles it. You shall have the honor of driving my restaurant every night for the rest of your life. I'll pay you well, but you're on your own for health insurance. I'm still on my parents' plan, so . . ."

"No can do," Knuckles said. "I've been avoidin' a real job fer years now. I don't like havin' t' show up on time t' things."

"You're hired!"

"I don't wanna be hired."

"Too late. I already hired you."

"Then I quit."

"You can't quit, not without two weeks' notice."

"Fine. This is my two weeks' notice."

"Fine. In two weeks (from the day we open), you may begin the process of finding a qualified replacement. In the meantime, I expect your best efforts. No lollygagging. No back talk. No drinking on the job. Got it?"

"*Fine.*" Knuckles scratched his bald scalp. "What jus' happened?"

At the back end of the cabin, Zoey opened a narrow door that led outside. Five-ish feet away, in the front end of Trolley 2, was another door. Zoey reached across the gap, opened the door, and hopped on over.

The inside of Trolley 2 looked the same as the inside of Trolley 1, minus a driver's box. Zoey glided through the cabin with outstretched arms. "This will be the dining parlor. I'll put tables on both sides so diners can look out the windows while they eat. Deuces on the right. Four-tops on the left. For parties of five or more, we'll push tables together."

Dallin hopped aboard Trolley 2. "How you gonna get your food from the kitchen in One to the dining parlor in Two?"

Zoey shrugged. "Hop across, I guess."

Knuckles hopped aboard too, saying, "Not while the trolleys 'r in motion, you're not. One slip and ya'd be roadkill."

"Plan B, then," Zoey said. "Dal, get me a price on those 'Beam me up, Scotty' things from *Star Trek*."

"On it." Dallin took out his phone and thumbed around online. "Can't. Not invented yet."

Zoey gave a disappointed sigh. "There goes *that* childhood fantasy. What about those Vanishing Cabinets from Harry Potter?"

Dallin thumbed around some more. "Can't. Borgin and Burkes closed in oh-five. The only people with Cabinets now are Death Eaters."

"Hey, Knuckles, know any Death Eaters?"

Knuckles said, "All ya gotta do is install some big windows at the ends o' both trolleys. Ya can stand in One, reach through the windows, 'n hand off yer food to a server in Two."

"I'd rather have Vanishing Cabinets," Zoey said.

"An' I'd rather not be the subject o' fourteen restraining orders," Knuckles said, "but ya can't always get whatcha want."

Dallin said, "Dude, you gotta join a church or something."

They moved to Trolley 3.

"This will be the live music room," Zoey said. "Valentine & the Night Owls will go on a stage here. I'll put tables here and here and here. People can watch the band while they drink Italian sodas and munch on Fried Avocado Rolls."

"Are you sure your mom will play?" Dallin said. "She's not too thrilled with your decision to start a restaurant."

"She's a musician," Zoey said. "She'd play inside an F6 tornado if there was an audience."

Dallin pointed to a closet at the rear of the cabin. "What's in there?"

The closet had a red door with a brass handle. Zoey

opened the door. Inside was a long metal lever jutting out of the floor.

"What do you think that does?" Zoey said.

Not one to pass up a good lever-pulling opportunity, Dallin scooted into the closet, took the lever in both hands, and pulled hard. The floorboards rumbled. Unseen gears shifted and shrieked. Dallin pushed the lever back to its original position, and the rumbling and shrieking stopped.

Dallin looked crestfallen. "I was hoping candy would come out."

"It's the emergency brake," Knuckles said. "If the driver's brakes stop working, ya pull that puppy and the trolleys'll screech to a stop."

Zoey looked around the cabin, her eyes twinkling with joy. "Okay, Knuckles, let's talk turkey. How much will it cost to fix up these trolleys, make one into a kitchen, one into a dining parlor, and one into a jazz club?"

Knuckles rubbed two fingers over a tattoo of an eight ball on his wrist. "Fully furnished?"

"Oh yes. I'm talking ovens, sinks, walk-in, cupboards, tables, chairs, lights, the whole shebang."

"Forty g's," Knuckles said.

"Time frame?"

"Two weeks."

"I'll pay half now, half when the job's done. Deal?"

Knuckles cleared his throat. It sounded like a fork in a garbage disposal. "Before I commit t' anything, I need yer word on a few things."

"Anything."

"One, ya gotta stay in school—"

"Easy."

"An' get straight As."

"Come again?"

"Straight As or I'm out."

"Fine. I'll get straight As."

"Two, ya can't run away from home at the age o' sixteen t' join a biker gang."

"Never crossed my mind."

"Three, if you're ever stranded in Nova Scotia, and yer buddies dare ya t' get a Darth Vader tattoo on yer lower back, you'll say no."

"These demands are getting weirdly specific."

"Lastly, when ya wreck yer Harley in front o' an old chapel in rural Kansas, and a pretty, young Presbyterian takes ya in, 'n nurses your wounds, 'n understands ya like no one ever has or ever will, 'n she begs ya t' leave yer biker gang, marry 'er, 'n spend the rest of yer days on a picturesque zucchini farm, you'll say yes. . . ." Knuckles sniffled. "I got sumthin' in my eye."

Dallin shook his head. "Dude, get a grip."

Zoey said, "We have a deal, then?"

Knuckles wiped a single tear from his chiseled cheek. "We got a deal."

The Pepper & the Bill

Zoey slept in until 7:30 a.m. Refreshed, she rolled out of bed, threw on her black-and-pink bathrobe, and went downstairs for a bowl of Cookie Crisp. (No chef, no matter how distinguished, is above Cookie Crisp.)

Her father was at the kitchen table, in a robe and slippers, sipping black coffee and reading a newspaper. (A newspaper is like a laptop with news on it, only it's made of paper. And if you press your finger on a word or picture to learn more about it, nothing happens. They were popular in the 1990s.)

"Get this," Gershwin said, tapping his forefinger on the column he was reading. "The hottest pepper in the world is called the Trinidad moruga scorpion. It measures two million units on the Scoville heat scale, whatever that is. There's a guy in town who sells them. He has to handle them with tongs because the pepper's juices would burn his fingers."

"That's one hot pepper," Zoey said.

Gershwin sipped his coffee. "According to this, the Trinidad doesn't burn much at first. It's tart and sweet.

Almost sour. The burn starts small and grows, like cancer, getting worse and worse until your entire head is numb. Its burn is persistent too. You could drink out of the Arctic Ocean, and the burn wouldn't go away. Only one thing stops the burning: mayonnaise."

"Mayonnaise?"

"A spoonful of mayo helps the burning go down. Otherwise, the burning lasts for weeks. People have died from it. The CIA wants to use it to fight terrorism."

Valentine loped into the kitchen, dressed in running shoes, spandex, a Windbreaker, and enough sweat to fill Sunset Reservoir.

"Good run?" Gershwin said.

Valentine gave an out-of-breath nod before dropping a stack of mail on the table. "Zoey, the one on top is for you."

While Valentine scoured the fridge for something cold to drink, Zoey picked up the envelope. No return address. *Huh.* She tore open the envelope, took out a one-page letter, and read aloud:

Dear Zoey Kate,

THIS IS A BILL

Loan origination fee:	*$4,000*
Pre-interest fee:	*$2,000*
Post-interest fee:	*$2,000*
Shipping & handling fee:	*$2,000*
Total Amount Due:	*$10,000*

You must pay the amount due immediately or incur the wrath of Mulberry Bank.

Warmest regards,

Miss Canela Lemon, Loan Officer
Mulberry Bank
272 Bay St., San Francisco, CA 94106

The letter trembled in Zoey's hands. "This can't be right. Miss Lemon said the first payment wasn't due until January and it would only be five hundred bucks."

Twisting the lid off a jug of orange juice, Valentine shook her head, saying, "I knew something like this would happen."

"This is why you should never do business with someone named after a fruit," Gershwin said. "One time I went to a chiropractor named Dr. Grape. I still can't turn my head all the way to the right." He turned his head twenty degrees. "See?"

Zoey shoved the letter into her pocket. "I have to get to the bank. Who can give me a ride?"

"Not me," said Gershwin. "I'm teaching an orchestration workshop at nine thirty. CCSF, other side of town."

"Mom?"

Valentine finished a long swig of orange juice. "Can't. Errands."

"Fine," Zoey said. "I'll walk."

Little Chef, Big Money (Um . . . Again)

 Zoey swept into Miss Lemon's office and slapped the bill onto the desk. "This better be a mistake!"

Leaning back in her cushy leather chair, Miss Lemon raised a turquoise mug of steaming herbal tea (Peach Tranquility, Zoey couldn't help but notice) and drew a long, slow sip. "Good morning, Zoey. I've been expecting you. Please, have a seat."

"I prefer to stand."

"Suit yourself." With her thumb and forefinger, Miss Baker picked at the tea string on the rim of her mug. "Have you come to pay the ten thousand dollars you owe, or have you come to argue? Wait, wait. Don't tell me. *Argue*."

Zoey picked up the bill, shook it, and slammed it down on the desk again. (She needed something to do with her hands.) "You never said anything about extra fees."

"I didn't think I needed to. After all, Zoey, you know everything." Miss Lemon's lips twitched like she was suppressing a smile.

"You're enjoying this," Zoey said. "Why?"

Miss Lemon set her mug on the desk. "The president of

Mulberry Bank paid me a personal visit yesterday. He said he wanted to inform me, in person, that the bank's health insurance policy wouldn't cover my recent lobotomy."

"Ooh," Zoey said brightly. "How was the baklava?"

Miss Lemon looked confused. "Who said anything about baklava?"

"You did."

"No I didn't."

"You went to Greece, right?" Zoey said. "You can't visit Greece and not try the baklava. That's like going to Turkmenistan and not trying the *shurpa*."

"A lobotomy," Miss Lemon said, "is a surgical procedure to remove a person's brain." She mimed cutting open the top of her skull with scissors.

"So . . . no baklava?"

"The bank president said I must've had a lobotomy because . . ." Miss Lemon cringed like she was recalling a traumatic event from her childhood. ". . . because only a brainless idiot would lend fifty thousand dollars to an aspiring twelve-year-old restaurateur."

"Did you tell him I'm a culinary genius?"

"No."

"Want me to talk to him?"

"He almost fired me." Miss Lemon looked panicked, like a firing was still a possibility. She sipped her tea. It calmed her down a little. "I had to plead to keep my job. I was on my hands and knees, like a dog begging for table scraps. I've never been so humiliated."

Zoey scratched an itch on the back of her neck. "If I didn't know better, I'd say you blame *me* for this."

"I do blame you for this."

"I didn't force you to do anything."

"You tricked me! You came in an hour before lunch, when you knew I'd be at my hungriest. You fed me a delicious chocolate truffle to pique my appetite, with a touch of jalapeño to pique my curiosity. Then, at your house, you blurred my senses with your tasty Balsamic Pear Ravioli and Fried Banana Fondue. I was in no state to make important financial judgments."

"So these extra fees are, what, your revenge?"

Holding the mug in both hands, Miss Lemon breathed in the rising steam. "Mmm. Yummy."

Zoey planted her index finger on the bill, pointing at the loan origination fee. "Four grand? A bit steep, don't you think?"

"A legitimate amount, considering the risk we've taken on you."

Zoey tapped the next line on the bill. "What the mustard is pre-interest?"

"Pre-interest is the fee you pay us before you pay us interest."

"Never heard of it."

"It's new."

"Sounds made-up."

"It's very new."

Zoey moved her finger to the next charge. "Post-interest?"

"That's the fee you pay us after you pay us interest."

"But I haven't paid any interest yet."

"We require post-interest payments in advance."

Zoey pointed at the final charge. "Shipping and handling? You haven't shipped or handled anything."

"We sent you this bill, didn't we?"

"I don't have ten thousand dollars," Zoey said.

"Correction," said Miss Lemon. "You have *fifty* thousand dollars."

"I already spent forty. I need the other ten for ingredients and supplies."

Miss Lemon paled. "You spent forty thousand dollars in one day?"

"I don't mess around."

Zoey and Miss Lemon stared at each other, like they were playing chess and they'd forgotten whose move it was. Until Zoey said, "Listen, I'd pay you if I could but I can't. I lost my checkbook and the cash is, um . . ." Zoey glanced down. ". . . tied up."

"It's in your boot, isn't it?"

"How'd you . . . ?"

"You looked down."

"Did not."

"There. You did it again."

"When?"

"Just now."

Zoey wanted to scream. "These fees are absurd. I won't pay them."

"You have to pay them."

"I refuse."

"You can't refuse."

"I refuse to accept I can't refuse."

"Suit yourself."

"I refuse to suit my— Wait, what?"

Miss Lemon grinned. It was not a nice grin. It was a sly, conniving, *I've-already-got-your-money-you-just-don't-know-it-yet* grin. (If you've ever said the words, "So all I gotta do is knock those three bottles over and I win that giant teddy bear?" you've seen it.) "If you refuse to pay, Zoey, then I can't force you."

"I sense a 'but' coming."

"But our lawyers can."

"There it is."

"We call them the pit bulls," Miss Lemon said with relish. (The emotion, not the hot-dog topping.) "If you refuse to pay, the pit bulls will sink their legal fangs into your skinny neck, make you bleed money. By the time they're done with you, ten grand will seem a mere trifle."

Zoey did not like her options. She felt like one of those plane crash survivors you read about: stranded in a jungle, desperate, wounded, and starving, forced to choose between eating a handful of poisonous berries or a dead flight attendant.

Seething, she reached into her right boot, pulled out a wad of hundred-dollar bills from her sock, and slapped it down on the desk. "There. Ten thousand. We done?"

"For now."

Zoey stormed out of the office, onto Bay Street. The sun was bright and warm. The placid breeze carried smells of carrotwood and ginkgo trees. At a sidewalk café across the street, folks enjoyed fresh coffee, clam omelets, and croissant French toast, and laughed at each other's jokes. A teenage girl and her boyfriend strolled past Zoey. The girl rested her head on her boyfriend's shoulder, like that was comfortable somehow.

The weather, the pleasant smells, the happy brunchers, young people in love: it was all wrong. *How can anyone be*

happy at a time like this? Don't they know I'm in the mid-
dle of a crisis?

Her phone rang. She answered. *"Oui?"*

"Yo, it's Knuckles. I'm calling about the trolleys. We got a problem."

"What kind of problem?"

Knuckles cleared his gravelly throat. "A big problem."

The Big Problem

 For the most part, the trolleys looked fantastic. Gone were the dents and chips. Gone were the cracked windows and cobwebs. Fresh coats of red, black, and gold paint glistened in the noonday sun. New windows looked shiny and spotless. Glass chandeliers and plush red carpet gave the dining trolleys an air of luxury and elegance.

There was something missing, however.

"Why aren't the wheels on?" Zoey said, placing her hand on Trolley 1's bare front axle.

"We put wheels on," Knuckles said, "but your fancy walk-in fridge and three stainless-steel ovens are too heavy. They crushed the wheels."

"So get stronger wheels."

Knuckles wiped grease off his fingers with an oily rag. "We tried that. There's only one company in the world that makes wheels strong enough and big enough for your trolleys. The wheels are solid titanium, and they ain't cheap."

"How much?"

"Five."

"Only five bucks?"

"Five thousand."

Zoey's heart sank like an uncooked potato in a pot of gravy. "Expensive day."

A gust of wind blew trash and debris across the junkyard floor. A crumpled plastic sack caught on Zoey's boot. She shook her foot. The bag came loose and tumbled away.

"There has to be another way," Zoey said.

"There is," Knuckles said. "Downgrade your kitchen appliances. Lose the anvil and fish tank and fire pit. Get lighter stuff."

"No way. I'm a professional chef. I need professional appliances."

"Then ya need another five grand."

"And how am I supposed to do that?"

"Whatever ya do, ya better do it soon. The company only has three sets of wheels left. That's one set for each trolley. If the company sells one more set, your trolleys ain't goin' nowhere."

Rainy Days Diner

Rainy Days Diner was a sad-people magnet. It shared a building with a divorce court, a Prozac pharmacy, a global warming research center, Supercuts, and a clinic for euthanizing ugly puppies. A sign on the diner's front door read NO SHAME, NO SORROW, NO SERVICE.

Inside, the walls were decorated with framed photos of grubby children standing in breadlines during the Great Depression. Wall-mounted TVs ran footage of the polar ice caps melting set to the music of Radiohead's "How to Disappear Completely."

The waitress, who dressed like Wednesday from *The Addams Family*, sat behind the counter, reading *Human Extinction Weekly* and stroking a taxidermy piranha.

Zoey sat at the counter, drowning her sorrows in a triple hot-fudge brownie sundae. When her spoon scraped the bottom of the bowl, the waitress said, "Anything else, lonesome?"

"Got ten grand?" Zoey said.

"A basset hound ate my cat," the waitress said. It was a

weird thing to say, but, hey, that's the kind of talk you hear at Rainy Days Diner.

The front door opened. In walked a middle-aged man with mocha skin and thinning black hair. He wore a gray uniform with button epaulets on the shoulders. A plaque on his left breast pocket read:

JAMBALAYA BARBOS, TOUR GUIDE, ALCATRAZ PRISON

Jambalaya took a seat at the counter, two stools down from Zoey. "Gimme one hundred hot dogs and a big glass of water," he told the waitress.

The waitress didn't even look up from her magazine. "You need a new hobby, dude."

"This time won't be like last time." Jambalaya patted his belly. "The machine is primed and ready for action."

The waitress sulked off to the kitchen, muttering something about "a heart attack" and "the depravation of humanity."

Jambalaya straightened his back and neck and placed his palms on the counter. He began to breathe in short, rapid bursts like a deep-sea diver preparing for a plunge.

Zoey swallowed a mouthful of hot fudge. "Hey, you okay?"

Jambalaya nodded.

"Why are you breathing like that?"

Jambalaya shook his head.

"Panic attack?"

Jambalaya shook his head.

"Allergic reaction to something?"

Jambalaya shook his head.

"Alien's gonna pop out of your chest?"

Jambalaya shook his head.

Minutes later, the waitress returned from the kitchen holding a glass of water and a tray of one hundred hot dogs stacked in a pyramid. *(I wonder how many days those have been under a heat lamp. . . .)* She placed the tray and glass on the counter. "If you blow chunks, do it outside." She tromped back into the kitchen.

Jambalaya pulled a stopwatch from his pocket. "Hey . . ." *Breath. Breath.* ". . . you got . . ." *Breath. Breath.* ". . . three minutes?"

Zoey looked at the pyramid of hot dogs. "You're gonna eat a hundred hot dogs in three minutes?"

"I . . ." *Breath. Breath.* ". . . hope so."

Zoey accepted the stopwatch. "This I gotta see."

"Count . . ." *Breath. Breath.* ". . . to three . . ." *Breath. Breath.* ". . . then press . . ." *Breath. Breath.* ". . . the green button."

"One . . . two . . . three." Zoey started the stopwatch.

Jambalaya folded a hot dog in half and crammed it into his mouth. While he chewed, he dipped a second hot dog into the glass of water. Swallowing the first hot dog, he thrust the soggy second hot dog into his mouth. While he chomped on the second hot dog, he dunked a third hot dog into the glass of water.

Jambalaya carried on in this fashion until, three minutes and forty-two hot dogs later, the stopwatch beeped and Zoey declared, "Time."

Red-faced and sweating, Jambalaya plonked his head

down on the counter and groaned. "I'll never move out of my parents' basement."

Zoey set the stopwatch on the counter. "Parents' basement?"

Jambalaya produced a paper flyer, handed it to Zoey. The flyer read:

25th ANNUAL
"HOT DOG" EATING CONTEST
WINNER GETS $10,000
Saturday, 10 a.m. @ AT&T Park, Center Field
$300 entry fee. Nonrefundable, even if you puke.
Sponsored by PETA

Zoey scoffed. "This is a joke, right? PETA is the animal rights people. Why would they sponsor a hot-dog eating contest?"

"It's no joke," said Jambalaya. "Last year, a guy ate seventy-two hot dogs and won ten grand. I was there. I saw it."

Whoosh. A spark of hope. "Can anyone enter?"

"Anyone with three hundred . . ." Jambalaya's cheeks and eyeballs swelled up like water balloons.

"You better go outside."

Clamping both hands over his mouth, Jambalaya sprinted out of the diner. As the front door swung closed behind him, Zoey heard the epic *SPLASH!* of vomit hitting pavement.

"Good luck with that," she hollered. It was the least she could do. "I'll just . . ." Zoey slipped the flyer into her skirt pocket. ". . . keep this."

I Say "Hot Dog," You Say "What the . . . ?"

 Zoey was not a baseball fan. She found the game slow and trivial. She could not understand how anyone could be so in love with such an underwhelming sport. And yet, as she stood on Giants stadium's dusty pitcher's mound, taking the place in—the arena seating, the mammoth scoreboard, the dugouts, the diamond, the bases, the smell of mowed grass, the thought of whacking a fastball over the fence into McCovey Cove—even she had to admit: *This is pretty cool.*

Competitive-eating fans crowded the stands and field. The PETA main stage was center field. Speaker towers stood on both sides of the platform, crowned by an epic rainbow of red, white, and blue balloons. A Santana cover band occupied the stage, playing "Oye Como Va" for a herd of dancing hippies.

Per their plans, Dallin met Zoey on the pitcher's mound at noon. The first words out of Dallin's mouth were:

"What—the heck—is that?"

Zoey froze, thinking maybe she had a huge, scary bug on her somewhere. "What the heck is what?"

Dallin pointed an accusing finger at her. *"That."*

"What, my face?"

"Your *jacket*." He said the word "jacket" the way a detective says, "It was *murder*."

"It's chilly. I wore my dad's old jacket. So what?"

"It's an Oakland Raiders jacket." Dallin spat, as if the words had left a bad taste in his mouth.

"So?"

"So the Raiders are evil incarnate."

"You say that about every team that's not the 49ers."

"But the Raiders are the evilest," Dallin insisted. "Before every game, they chant 'Death to America' and strangle a bald eagle."

"I doubt that."

Dallin yanked on her sleeve. "Take it off."

"No. I'm cold."

Dallin hadn't looked this betrayed since the time his mom snuck a 3 Musketeers from his Halloween stash. "We can't be friends anymore." He headed for the dugouts.

"Wait. What if I turn it inside out?"

Dallin stopped. He looked around to make sure no one was watching. "I'll allow it. Hurry."

Zoey took off her jacket, turned it inside out, and put it on again. "Happy now?"

Dallin let out a loud, forced laugh. Then, in a loud-enough-for-everyone-to-hear voice, exclaimed, *"FUNNY PRANK, Z, PRETENDING TO BE A RAIDERS FAN! WE ALL KNOW YOU BLEED RED AND GOLD. HA-HA! NATURAL LAUGHTER!"* He leaned in close. "We never speak of this again."

* * *

As Zoey and Dallin weaved through the unwashed mass toward the stage, Zoey took out a neon green plastic wristband and fastened it to Dallin's wrist. "This bracelet is your ticket to the contest. It cost me three hundred bucks. Don't lose it."

"So all I gotta do is eat more hot dogs than everyone else?"

"That's it."

"Sounds easy."

"Way easy."

Los Siete Carlitos finished their song and walked offstage. A man with curly red hair, white sunglasses, and a Barry Bonds jersey appeared. Holding a gold microphone to his lips, he threw back his head and howled like a wolf. The crowd howled in response.

"Hey, hey, hey!" the man said. "This is DJ Wolfman from ninety-eight FM, coming to you live from AT&T Park. We're getting ready for PETA's Twenty-fifth Annual 'Hot Dog' Eating Contest. Get onstage, contestants. It's showtime."

Ten contestants climbed onto the stage. Dallin was the only kid. A woman in a headset arranged the contestants in a straight line, shoulder to shoulder.

Arms folded, elbows resting on the stage, Zoey gave Dallin an encouraging smile. Dallin didn't smile back. He had his game face on.

Stagehands placed podiums in front of each contestant. Each podium held a pyramid of a hundred hot dogs and a glass of water. DJ Wolfman said, "Ladies and gents, give it up for our returning champ, Big Masi."

The man next to Dallin raised his mighty fists into the

air. He was Samoan and seven feet tall, with a belly so big he looked pregnant. He had bushy white dreadlocks and a ratty beard that hung to his chest. He wore a Grateful Dead T-shirt, a Samoan-print lavalava, and Birkenstock sandals.

"It's simple, folks. Each contestant has three minutes to eat as many hot dogs as he or she can. Whoever eats the most wins. Any questions? If so, you're a moron. Clocks ready, judges, three minutes starts in five, four, three, two . . . *STUFF YOUR FACES, PIGGIES!*"

Cheers rang from the crowd as the ten competitors commenced packing their mouths with hot dogs.

Dallin grimaced like he'd bitten into a cat's tail. He spat out a wad of goopy bread and masticated brown stuff. "Nasty!"

"Dal! What're you doing? Eat the hot dog!"

"This ain't a hot dog," Dallin said.

"It's a tofu dog!" DJ Wolfman said. "Meat is murder, so we make our hot dogs from all-natural vegetarian ingredients!"

Dallin backed away from the podium, mortified.

Big Masi was on his tenth hot dog.

Zoey cried out, "Just eat it!"

Dallin took another step back. "No way! It's unnatural."

"I cook with tofu all the time!"

"Not in hot dogs, you don't!"

"Tofu is a delicacy in the Orient!"

"This is America!" Dallin placed a hand over his heart. "We make hot dogs the way nature intended, with meat and stuff. If I eat that, I'll betray my heritage!"

Zoey had to clap her hands against the sides of her head to keep her brain from exploding. "You're killing me, Dal!"

Big Masi was on his twenty-fifth hot dog.

"One minute down," DJ Wolfman announced. "Two to go."

Zoey wasn't about to lose ten thousand dollars on account of some coagulated soybean curds. "Dal, if you don't start inhaling those tofu dogs, I'll . . ." Her mind raced. *How do I get this kid to start scarfing, already?*

Then she remembered.

The jacket.

". . . I'll become a Raiders fan!"

Dallin shuddered like he'd been shot in the stomach. "You wouldn't."

"Go silver and black!"

"Not funny, Z."

Big Masi was on his thirtieth hot dog.

Zoey tapped her chin, pretending to consider a provocative new idea. "I think I'll invent a new drink. I'll call it Raider-ade."

Dallin trembled. "Don't say that name!"

"The Raiders are way better than the 49ers."

Dallin wiped his fingers over his eyes. Was he crying? "You're crossing a line, Z!"

"I wonder if the Raiders' defensive end has a son my age . . ."

"*AGHHHHHHH!*" Dallin threw himself at his pile of tofu dogs. His hands moved between the tray and his mouth in a blur. Four at a time, he sucked down tofu dogs with the efficiency of an industrial vacuum cleaner.

Big Masi, who was leading the other contestants at forty-six dogs, took notice of Dallin's hustle and increased his intake to two dogs at a time. Dallin increased his intake to five hot dogs at a time, smashing them tight in his fist before stuffing them into his mouth.

"You better watch your back, Big Masi," said DJ Wolfman. "The kid is gaining on ya!"

Big Masi increased his intake to four dogs at once. This tactic slowed him down because he couldn't close his mouth all the way.

Zoey clapped and hooted. "Keep going, Dal!"

Dallin pressed on, smashing and chomping and swallowing like a high-speed wood chipper.

"I don't believe it!" DJ Wolfman said. "The kid and Big Masi are tied at sixty tofu dogs! With one minute to go and ten grand at stake, who will be this year's winner?"

Big Masi's face turned eggplant purple as he struggled to choke down three dogs at once. In this endeavor, he was no match for Dallin.

Dallin didn't slow. He stopped chewing altogether, gulping down tofu dogs like they were Jell-O.

Zoey cupped her hands around her mouth. "Almost there, Dal! Keep going!"

"Thirty seconds to go," DJ Wolfman said. "The kid is leading the pack at eighty-five tofu dogs. What's that kid's name, anyway?"

Zoey called out, *"DALLIN CARAWAY!"*

The crowd began to chant. *"DAL-LIN! DAL-LIN! DAL-LIN!"*

Dallin stopped and waved at his newfound fans.

"KEEP GOING, DAL!" Zoey hollered, barely audible above the chanting crowd.

Dallin resumed stuffing hot dogs into his mouth.

"Ten seconds left," said DJ Wolfman. "Can Dallin hold his lead? Ten . . . nine . . . eight . . ."

Dallin swallowed his one hundredth hot dog. Big Masi ate as fast as he could, trailing at a meager ninety dogs.

"Seven . . . six . . ."

Having finished all the hot dogs on his tray, Dallin swiped three dogs from Big Masi's tray. The crowd laughed and clamored.

"Five . . . four . . ."

Dallin tossed a tofu dog high into the air, caught it in his mouth, and with outstretched arms sucked it down in one gulp.

"Three . . . two . . . *WE HAVE A NEW CHAMPION!*"

Red, yellow, and orange confetti shot over the stage like fireworks. Triumphant orchestral music blared from the speakers. Big Masi bent over, pulled his beard to the side, and vomited onto his Birkenstocks.

(Miles away, Jambalaya Barbos lay on a futon in his parents' basement, clutching a copy of *How to Win Friends and Influence People* and sobbing.)

Zoey climbed onto the stage. She flung her arms around Dallin's shoulders and kissed him hard on the cheek. "You rock, Dal! I owe you one."

Dallin blushed. "You owe me ten thousand, actually."

DJ Wolfman presented Dallin with a check the size of a highway billboard. Putting his arm around Dallin, DJ Wolfman spoke into his microphone. "Dallin Caraway, you just outate nine grown adults and won ten thousand dollars. What are you going to do now?"

DJ Wolfman held the microphone to Dallin's lips.

"Puke," Dallin said. "Maybe pass out."

Zoey walked to the back of the stage, took out her cell phone, and dialed Knuckles.

Knuckles answered. "Yeah."

Zoey stuck her finger in her left ear to block out the noises onstage. "Hey, Knuckles, what's the name of that company that makes those titanium tires? I'm ready to make a purchase."

The Calm Before the Awesome

Two weeks later-ish, on a warm, breezy Friday evening, in a sleepy alley near Fisherman's Wharf, three trolleys stood in a straight line, their pristine facades boasting fresh coats of red, black, and gold, their sturdy titanium wheels glimmering in the tangerine dusk.

In Trolley 1, the engine rumbled like a sleeping grizzly bear waking up from a long winter of hibernation. The rumbling made the floor vibrate, but only a little. Thanks to a thorough *mise en place*, Zoey's walk-in was stocked with fresh meats, produce, milks, creams, cheeses, barrels of whole grains, flours, sugars, yeasts, oils, spices, and a dozen pies and cakes made from scratch that morning. Her three conventional ovens were preheated to 350, 400, and 425 degrees, respectively. Flames glowed in the fire pit and brick oven. Pots of water boiled on the stovetop. Live crustaceans, plucked from San Francisco Bay, wallowed in the large saltwater tank. Racks of pork and beef ribs simmered in the smoker, tender, medium rare, and ready to serve.

In Trolley 2, bejeweled chandeliers cast a luxurious off-white glow upon two rows of tables draped in fine black silk. Silverware and wineglasses sparkled like diamonds. The red-velvet-cupcake-colored carpet was so plush and soft a queen could've slept on it and counted herself lucky.

Trolley 3 looked and felt like a nightclub. A small stage occupied one end. Tall tables and barstools occupied the other end. Between them lay a low-lit, hardwood dance floor.

Onstage, Valentine & the Night Owls warmed up. Fat Jo tightened his hi-hat, making the cymbals crisp and tight. Monk ran scales covering the full range of the piano. Four sat on a stool, holding up a massive acoustic four-string, and reading *Men Are from Mars, Women Are from Venus.* Bird adjusted his saxophone's mouthpiece. Valentine put on ChapStick, raised her trumpet to her lips, and played the opening lick from Dizzy Gillespie's "Salt Peanuts."

Also in Trolley 3, wearing a white hat with a gold band and an all-black suit, shirt, and tie, Gershwin sifted through a stack of leather-bound menus, inserting 4 x 4 adverts for tonight's dessert special: Caramel Blackberry Quesadillas with Pineapple Cream Cheese Filling.

Knuckles stood in the darkest corner, picking a scab on his wrist.

Zoey sat on a stool in a different corner, eyes closed, meditating, getting into her creative space. Dallin sat on a stool next to her, watching videos of the 49ers' 1989 and 1994 Super Bowl wins. He wore a black suit jacket, white shirt, black tie, black sweatpants, and red Nikes. The sweats and Nikes were free of holes, tears, and grass stains, so Zoey let them slide.

At five till seven-ish, Zoey arose, put on her black toque with red trim, fastened two rows of red buttons on her otherwise black chef jacket, and tied on her sparkly gold apron. She strode to the center of the dance floor and clapped twice. "Line up, troops. It's almost game time."

Dallin, Gershwin, and the band didn't line up, exactly, but they did gather around to listen.

"Tonight is a big night for me," Zoey said, "and I'm honored to be sharing it with all of you."

Seated on a barstool, Fat Jo clapped his drumsticks together. "Hear, hear."

The others clapped too in an *I-guess-we're-supposed-to-clap-now* kind of way. (If you've ever been to a kids' piano recital, you've heard it.)

"Band," Zoey said, "I want you to start with a bang. Something big and fast and catchy and loud. Make the people in Oakland hear you."

The band members traded excited grins and glances.

"But," Zoey said, "once we got a full house, your job is to fade into the background. The headliner here is the food, not the music. You must create an ambience that relaxes people, at a volume they can talk over."

Excited grins and glances, gone.

"Fat Jo," Zoey said, "that means brushes, not sticks."

Fat Jo laid his sticks on the table. "Fine."

"And, Mom, no notes over high A."

Valentine flexed her pinkie against her trumpet's finger hook. "Fine."

"Dallin and Gershwin," Zoey said, "you're servers, not talk show hosts. Customers wanna spend time with friends and family, not you, so no chitchat. Your job is to take orders, run food, and be as inconspicuous as ninjas.

"When you approach a table, say, 'Good evening. My

name is such and such. What may I bring you to drink?'"

Gershwin raised his hand. "Should we say 'How are you?' first?"

"You already know how they're doing," Zoey said. "They're in my restaurant, so they're fabulous."

Dallin said, "That makes sense."

"If a customer asks if something on the menu is good, say, 'No . . .'"

Concerned looks.

"'. . . it's amazing.'"

Relieved nods.

"If a customer asks what you recommend, recommend the Chocolate-Covered Pork Chops. It's my signature dish, and my most expensive, so we wanna push that as hard as we can.

"If a customer orders a dish that's eighty-sixed . . ."

Dallin and Gershwin raised their hands.

"That means we've run out of ingredients for it."

Dallin and Gershwin lowered their hands.

"If a dish is eighty-sixed, don't apologize. Say, 'That dish is so popular we ran out already. Allow me to direct you to a menu item for more refined palates.' Then point to any item on the menu and gush over it."

Four said, "I cry in bed a lot."

Everyone stared at him.

Four's cheeks turned beet red. "Out loud?"

Bird placed a consoling hand on Four's sagging shoulder.

"Sorry," Four said. "Carry on."

Zoey said, "You may have noticed an absence of salt and pepper shakers on the tables. It's by design. Diners use salt and pepper to coax flavor out of bland food. My food is never bland, so salt and pepper shakers are never necessary.

"Now, a word about birthdays. If a customer says she's celebrating her birthday, you may congratulate her, but no singing. This a first-class restaurant, not a Chuck E. Cheese's."

Valentine raised her hand.

"Yes, Mom, you may quote the 'Happy Birthday' song in a trumpet solo."

Valentine lowered her hand.

Four said, "Out loud again?"

Since no one knew what Four was talking about, Bird said, "No, bro, that one was in your head."

"Lastly," Zoey said, "things may get stressful tonight. If I lose my temper and scream like a maniac and throw loud metallic objects, please remember: I'm a chef. That's what we do. Any questions?"

Four said, "Will there be women here tonight?"

Zoey said, "I should hope so."

Four and Bird bumped fists.

"Anyone else?" Zoey said.

Dallin raised his hand. "Next Wednesday, my team's got a scrimmage against Aptos MS. Will you come watch me?"

Zoey said, "Oh, is the coach gonna play you?"

Dallin's face turned whiter than clam chowder. Had her question merely embarrassed him, his face would have turned rhubarb pink. But she had done worse than embarrass him. She had humiliated him. In front of Knuckles, her parents, and the Night Owls, no less.

"Heck yeah, I'll be there!" Zoey said with enthusiasm,

hoping to divert from his embarrassment. "You're gonna be awesome. I'll scream my lungs out after every home run."

"Touchdown," Monk said.

"That too." Zoey winked at Dallin. His face returned to its normal color. "Anyone else?"

Knuckles cleared his throat. It sounded like a lawn mower running over barbed wire. "Anyone got a big metal hook I can borrow?"

Valentine's mama-bear instincts kicked in. "For the love of Louis, why do you need a big metal hook?"

Knuckles considered the question for a moment, then said, "Forget I said anything."

Zoey said, "Any other questions?"

Dallin raised his hand. "Hey, at my scrimmage, if I clobber the quarterback because I'm like a freaking hurricane on the field, and everyone's cheering for me, and I point at you on the sidelines like, 'That was for you, Z,' that'd be pretty cool, wouldn't it?"

"Um, sure, Dal."

Dallin tried to fist-bump Monk. Monk ignored him.

"Other questions?"

Knuckles cleared his throat again. This one sounded like a tank driving through a concrete wall. "Anyone got a big, heavy-duty duffel bag you're not using? Something you wouldn't mind having buried in the woods for a few years?"

Silence.

Everyone took small steps away from Knuckles, like they didn't feel safe standing next to him.

Zoey said, "Any other questions?"

Dallin and Four raised their hands.

Zoey said, "Any questions not about Dal's scrimmage?"

Dallin lowered his hand.

Zoey said, "Or women?"

Four lowered his hand.

No other hands went up.

Zoey said, "Dal, how's it coming with the speech we practiced?"

Dallin tapped the top of his head. "It's all in there."

Zoey put forth her right hand, fingers spread, palm down. "Bring it in."

Gershwin, Dallin, Knuckles, and the band huddled around Zoey, placing their hands atop hers.

"Shock the world on three," Zoey said. "One, two, three."

As one, they raised their hands into the air with a mighty shout. "Shock the world!"

Opening Night

Zoeylicious slowed to a stop at the corner of Jefferson and Hyde. A crowd of curious onlookers gathered at the curb.

Dallin stood in the doorway of Trolley 2 and held out his arms. "People of San Francisco, Zoeylicious is now open for business! Step on in for the lifetime of a dining experience! Wait, I mean . . ."

In Trolley 1, Zoey clapped a hand to her forehead.

Dallin looked down at his left hand. (He'd written his lines on his palm in case of, well, *this*.) "I mean, the dining experience of a lifferham . . . my hand's sweaty."

The people on the sidewalk responded with befuddled stares.

Dallin made an *eh-forget-it!* face. (If you've ever watched your uncle Bubba try to do a sit-up, you've seen it.) "You got mouths, we got food. Get on if you want some."

In Trolley 3, Valentine & the Night Owls launched into a lively rendition of Duke Ellington's "Take the A Train." Knuckles played with sticks, and Valentine went after those high As. More and more onlookers gathered on the sidewalk. Some clapped to the music. An elderly couple started dancing. Then, one by one, couple by couple, group by group, the onlookers stepped aboard Trolleys 2 and 3.

Zoey watched through the serving windows as Dallin ushered customers to tables and handed them menus. At the back of Trolley 2, a serving window aligned with another serving window in Trolley 3. Through these windows, Zoey could see Gershwin greeting customers and jotting down orders on a three-by-six order pad.

The driver's box door opened. Knuckles sat half turned, one hand on the steering wheel, the other hand holding open the door. "Go time?"

"Go time," Zoey said.

Knuckles pulled the compartment door closed. Stainless-steel light fixtures swayed overhead as Zoeylicious rolled forward.

From Trolley 2, Dallin reached through the serving windows into Trolley 1, his pudgy fingers clasping a wrinkled ticket. "Order's up."

Zoey accepted the ticket, read it.

1 POPEYE MANGO TIGER PRAHN KRAPS

CRAIPS RHYMES WITH DRAPES

Zoey chuckled. *Note to self: teach Dallin how to spell "papaya" and "prawn" and "crêpes."*

"Great work, Dal," she said.

Dallin gave a proud nod. "Knock 'em dead, Z." He trotted off to get more orders.

Zoey clipped the ticket to the board above the stoves. *Let's do this.*

She dashed to the other end of the kitchen. She plunged her hands into the saltwater tank. The icy cold produced goose bumps on her skin. Her fingers stiffened as they sifted past wriggling lobsters, crabs, and snails before locating a pair of foot-long tiger prawns. She drew the prawns out of the water. Their gangling legs scratched at her wrists.

Now for the unpleasant part.

Zoey placed one prawn on the counter. She took the other prawn's head in her left fist, its body in her right. In one swift motion, she bent her wrists in opposite directions like she was wringing out a wet rag. The prawn's shell went *crackle*, and its head popped off its spine.

Zoey tossed the head into the trash and laid the decapitated body on the counter. She picked up the second prawn and ripped off its head too.

With a fork and butter knife, Zoey de-shelled both prawns. She brushed a papaya glaze on the prawns' pale gray flesh. When the prawns hit the 400-degree griddle, they steamed and sizzled like bacon.

While the prawns cooked, Zoey poured a creamy almond-white batter onto the center of a round griddle. She placed a T-shaped wooden spreader at the center of the bubbling batter and twisted the T in her fingers, causing the batter to spread out in a flat circle. When the circle of batter reached twelve inches in diameter, Zoey swapped the T for a spatula. She flipped the crêpe and prawns like they were pancakes.

The cooking crêpe smelled like a waffle cone, only milkier. The prawns smelled like shrimp, naturally, and with their claws removed, who could tell the difference? (Prawns have claws on three of their ten legs; shrimp only have claws on two—a distinction so fascinating its remembrance sent chills up Zoey's spine.)

Zoey transferred the finished crêpe to a white glass plate. She spooned a dollop of homemade pineapple purée onto the center of the crêpe, then used the back of the spoon to streak the dollop evenly over the crêpe's smooth surface. Upon this citrusy bed Zoey laid the prawns, their flesh fluffy and white with pink stripes. Upon the prawns she laid mango strips, coconut flakes, cilantro, and a squeeze of lime juice. She folded up the sides of the crêpe so it resembled a pudgy burrito, sprinkled powdered sugar on top, and *voilà*! One Papaya Mango Tiger Prawn Crêpe.

Zoey placed the dish, ready to run, on the window pass. From Trolley 2, Dallin reached through the windows and took the plate. He served the dish to a man in a cranberry turban, sitting alone at Table 1. The man's fork cut through the crêpe like a hot knife through warm butter. The man raised the fork to his lips, blew on its steaming contents, and slotted the tines into his mouth. His eyebrows raised in delight, lifting his turban an inch.

Zoey smiled. *He loves it.*

Zoey's cell phone rang on her hip. She answered. "*Bonjour*, Gershwin."

"Hi-de-ho, Zoey. I need two Maple Cinnamon Crab Fajitas, two Coconut Lime Pheasant Arepas, two Boysenberry Vanilla Sodas, and two Strawberry Rhubarb Sodas."

"On it."

Zoey whirled about the kitchen, her hands busy, her mind juggling recipes and temperatures and cooking times.

When the fajitas, arepas, and sodas were ready, she passed them to Dallin in Trolley 2, who passed them to Gershwin in Trolley 3.

Zoeylicious cruised through Haight-Ashbury, Golden Gate Park, and the Presidios, stopping to pick up new customers and drop off full ones. Knuckles navigated with skill and grace, never accelerating or braking too fast, going slow around corners and avoiding potholes, so the ride was smoother than French vanilla pudding.

As twilight turned into night, and Zoeylicious cruised across the towering Golden Gate Bridge, the chilly breeze whispered through the trolleys' open windows, as gentle as good-night kisses. In response, the heaters in Trolleys 2 and 3 kicked on, keeping the dining parlors at a cozy seventy-two degrees. Behind them, in the distance, the lights of downtown San Francisco looked like millions of yellow lanterns hung upon the darkness.

Hours passed like minutes. Orders came in. Dishes went out. Customers ate like royalty and paid like gamblers. Zoeylicious was bringing in as much as two hundred dollars per table. If tonight was any indication of the future, Zoey would be a millionaire by the age of sixteen. Now the prospect of paying back fifty thousand dollars to Mulberry Bank didn't seem so daunting.

At two-ish a.m., Zoeylicious closed for the night. Knuckles parked Zoeylicious at the end of the Embarcadero on Fisherman's Wharf. The docks and piers were empty. The sea was quiet, its glassy surface reflecting the yellow moon. Knuckles joined Dallin, Gershwin, and Valentine & the Night Owls in Trolley 3 to relax, drink Italian sodas, munch on Foie Gras Paté with Brie on Toasted Baguettes, and talk about whatever it is guys talk about at two in the morning when there's a lady present.

Zoey, meanwhile, was in Trolley 2, seated at a four-top with a calculator and a pile of tickets and receipts. She had three envelopes: one marked "Dallin," one marked "Knuckles," and one marked "Valentine & the Night Owls." She packed each envelope with cash, licked them sealed, and deposited them in her apron pocket.

Then she counted the receipts: 151 dishes served. That's 151 customers plus the 330 who had already tried her cooking, for a grand total of 481.

She kicked off her purple Doc Martens, put her feet up on the table, and leaned back in her chair. Gazing out the window at the glimmering sea, she let out a slow, gratified sigh. *481 down. 6,999,999,519 to go.*

Not a bad start.

Game or Fame

Zoey stepped outside into the crisp morning air, rocking a white T-shirt with the words "GOOOOOO DALLIN!!!" hand-painted on the front. One side of her face was painted red. The other side was painted gold. Her hair was pulled up in a tight bun atop her head. The bun secured the base of a twelve-inch plastic field goal post with spinning green lights on top.

(Life lesson: Never google "What should I wear to a football game?" because you might end up looking like this.)

Zoeylicious was parked across the street, parallel to the sidewalk. Beyond the sidewalk rose a steep thirty-foot hill draped in leafy bushes and snaking vines.

For some reason, a limousine was parked at the rear of Zoeylicious. The engine was running. Three people—one woman and two men—were standing in the street, peeking through Trolley 3's speckless windows.

Zoey marched across the street. "May I help you?"

The woman turned to face Zoey. She wore sleek black clothes, big black sunglasses, and an Audrey Hepburn sun hat. "Hello, young lady. I'm looking for Chef Zoey Kate. Do you know if she lives around here?"

"She does." Zoey was hesitant to reveal her identity until she knew who these people were and what they wanted.

The two men faced her now too. One was clean-shaven with immaculate gray hair. He dressed like an executive: designer shoes, power slacks, collared shirt with cuff links. The other guy hadn't shaved or cut his hair in months. He dressed like a roadie for a rock band: ratty Ramones T-shirt with cutoff sleeves, chrome-studded belt, frayed jeans, combat boots.

"Do you know which house is hers?" asked Clean-Shaven.

Zoey pointed over her shoulder with her thumb. "That one."

Audrey Hepburn Hat said, "Oh, is she your mother?"

"She's *me*," Zoey said, annoyed by the woman's ageist presumptions.

Audrey Hepburn Hat's eyes scanned Zoey from head (er, goalpost) to toe.

"I don't normally dress like this," Zoey said.

Audrey Hepburn Hat nodded to the two men. Clean-Shaven turned and took out his phone. Roadie made for the limo.

Zoey said, "What's this about?"

Audrey Hepburn Hat smiled. Her gorgeous teeth were even straighter and whiter than Zoey's. "I beg your pardon, Chef." She extended her hand. "I'm Kim Chi, *New York Times*."

Zoey shook the reporter's hand with enthusiasm. *"Enchantée."*

"Likewise."

"What brings you to the West Coast?"

"Well . . ." Kim Chi sighed like she was tired. "We had intended to do a story on the history of Italian cuisine in San Francisco."

"Ooh, you *have* to meet my friend. His name is Chef Cannoli. His restaurant is La—"

"La Cucina di Cannoli, I know. I sat down with him yesterday. Three-hour interview."

"Did he do the kiss-you-on-the-cheek-to-say-hello thing?"

"He did." Kim Chi folded her arms and shivered. "A lot."

Roadie was unloading heavy-duty equipment boxes from the limo's trunk. Clean-Shaven was twelve feet away, back still turned, his phone to his ear. "Look, we'll shelve the Italian piece, go back to it later. This one's too hot to sit on. . . ."

"What's your interest in *my* restaurant?" Zoey asked. "It's not Italian."

"Your restaurant," said Kim Chi, "is the talk of the town. Who cares about old Italian restaurants when there's one of these . . ." Kim Chi motioned to the trolleys. ". . . and one of *you* . . ." She pointed to Zoey. ". . . on the scene? We've been tracking you down for three days now."

Turning, Clean-Shaven cupped his hand over his phone's mouthpiece. "Ya need a website, kid."

"Working on it." Zoey didn't bother mentioning that a team of skilled developers in Kandahar was hard at work on a website that would *smell* and *taste* like chocolate chip cookies. The technology was new. Development was slow.

Clean-Shaven went on, "We only found you because our driver passed your street on the way to the airport and I happened to look out the window."

"I'm happy you found me," Zoey said. "How can I be of service?"

Kim Chi said, "We'd love an interview."

"Awesome. I'm on my way to a scrimmage. Meet me here in two hours?"

Clean-Shaven said, "Our flight leaves in two and a half."

"What if you drove me to the football field, interviewed me on the way?"

Kim Chi said, "We prefer video interviews."

Clean-Shaven said, "Videos get more eyeballs."

Roadie returned from the limo, a pro-grade video camera in one hand, a box with a handle in the other. "We'll shoot in the kitchen. Sit-down Q and A. Quick and dirty. Natural light. Camera mic. Then a walk-through of cars two and three. I'll go handheld to save time. It's too bad we can't be there tonight. I'd love some action shots."

Too bad, indeed, Zoey thought, but for a different reason.

"Ya need a website, kid," Clean-Shaven said for the second time.

Kim Chi said to Clean-Shaven, "What if she cooks for us now?" Then, to Roadie: "You'd get your action shots."

Roadie looked at Zoey. "Can ya flambé?"

"Of course."

"How big can you get the flames?"

"An inch shy of the ceiling," Zoey said. She couldn't

shake the feeling that by answering these questions, she was committing to an interview.

Roadie looked at his colleagues. "I like it."

"Me too," Kim Chi said.

Clean-Shaven looked at Zoey. "Can ya lose the face paint and goalposts?"

This was it. Decision time.

Dallin's scrimmage or the *New York Times*?

Watch Dallin warm a bench for two hours . . . or take the publicity opportunity of a lifetime?

Be a friend. Or disappoint a friend.

Kim Chi folder her arms and arched her eyebrows. "Well . . . ?"

Zoey thought a moment more, then made her decision.

"I'll get cleaned up," she said.

She would explain it all to Dallin later. He would understand. He'd have to.

Gag Reflex

On Friday morning, July 10, the *New York Times* posted its twenty-two-minute video report titled "No Rules, No Limits: the Making of a 12-Year-Old Celebrity Chef."

Zoey sat cross-legged on her bed, dressed in black silk pajamas and a pink robe, watching the report on her iPad. She looked good on camera (not as good as Kim Chi, but good). The editors had spliced her interview to include only the sound bites of Zoey at her sharpest.

Fifteen minutes in, Zoey became annoyed at the report's focus on her age over her cooking. She took heart, though, when Kim Chi, perched on a black stool in a dimly lit New York studio, said the following:

The menu is progressive, intriguing, and a little bit insane. It boasts dishes like Bacon-Wrapped Pineapple Pheasant Shish Kebabs, Huckleberry Steak Tartare, and Blueberry Ratatouille Crisp with Garlic Chive Mashed Potatoes.

To the adventurous, I recommend the Chocolate-Covered Pork Chops. The chocolate sauce is similar to a mole, like Mexicans put on their chicken and pork, but with a heaviness characteristic of the chocolates of Switzerland and France. The meat is moist, tender, and grilled to perfection.

I don't know if there are other Chocolate-Covered Pork Chops in the world, but if there are then I promise you this: Chef Zoey's Chocolate-Covered Pork Chops are, without question, the world's greatest Chocolate-Covered Pork Chops.

The video cut to Chef Cannoli, seated in his kitchen, dressed in his finest whites. "Zoey Kate is a brave cook and a friend," he said.

The video cut to Zoey and Kim Chi strolling through Trolley 3, admiring Fat Jo's drum set. Then back to Kim Chi in the studio, saying:

If you're in San Francisco, and you see Zoeylicious roll by, hop aboard for the dining experience of a lifetime. Order the Chocolate-Covered Pork Chops, extra chocolate. From the New York Times, *I'm Kim Chi.*

Fade to black.

"Eh," Zoey said, "I've had better."

Had this been her first published review, she might've rolled onto her back, kicked her feet in the air, and shrieked with glee, but this wasn't her first review. Since its grand opening, Zoeylicious had received an average of three reviews per day, all of them positive, most of them glowing.

Though pleased, more or less, with the *New York Times*'s report, she worried about her relationship with Chef Cannoli. Kim Chi had interviewed him for three hours, after all. No chef, no matter how generous, would give a three-hour interview, get four seconds of screen time (endorsing another chef, no less), then whistle a merry tune.

On-screen, below the video, was the text copy of the complete Chef Zoey interview. Zoey tapped the Print button. On the dresser, a printer hummed to life, spitting out three pages of crisp, warm paper. Zoey set her iPad on the nightstand. She hopped off her bed and pinned them to the wall, adding to an ever-expanding mural of reviews.

Tucking her thumbs into her robe's pockets, she admired her "wall of fame," trying to derive a sense of satisfaction. But she couldn't. Despite rave reviews from the *San Francisco Chronicle*, *Bay Area Beatnik Weekly*, *Fog City Foodie*, *Eat. Purge. Repeat.*, and dozens of food bloggers, Zoey lacked a review from the critic who mattered most:

Royston Basil Boarhead, *Golden Gate Magazine*.

All in good time, she reminded herself.

There came a knock on Zoey's door. The knock was hard and clunky, so it hadn't come from Valentine or Gershwin. Valentine's knock was staccato yet graceful, like a trumpet. Gershwin's knock was smooth and steady like a walking bass. This hard, clunky knock could have only come from one person.

"Come in, Dal."

The door opened. Dallin strutted into the room with a boisterous "Ha-ha!" He wore aviator sunglasses. A

Bluetooth headset clung to one ear like a koala bear on a tree limb. Pressing a finger against the earpiece, Secret Service–style, he turned his back to Zoey, saying, "Sounds good, baby. Talk later. *Ciao bello.*"

"*Ciao bello?*" Zoey said. "When did you become the Renaissance man?"

With dramatic flourish, Dallin turned and whipped off his sunglasses. "Oh? Hey, Z. I did not see you there."

"It's my *bedroom*," Zoey said.

Dallin hung his sunglasses on the neck of his 49ers T-shirt. (Today's shirt was a Super Bowl XXIV champions commemorative, white, with caricatures of Steve Young and Jerry Rice holding trophies.) "Anyways, I bet you're wondering why you haven't seen me in a while."

"I see you every night."

"At your restaurant, yeah. But not here at your house. I haven't been here in nine days."

"Keeping a tally, I see."

"Anyways, I've been crazy busy. I got so much cool stuff going on, I shouldn't even be here right now. I should be . . ." He waved one hand in the air as if grasping for a lost thought. ". . . you know, stuff."

"Uh-huh." Zoey sat down on her bed. "Hey, wanna see the video the *New York Times* did on—"

"Guess how many contacts I have in my phone."

"Um . . ."

Dallin held out his arms like those tough guys you see in rap videos. "Twenty-six. Bam!"

"O . . . kay . . . ?"

"I could call any one of them, right now, and they'd be like, 'Yo, D, how's it going, brah?' Like that. And I'd be like, 'Wuzzup?' And they'd be like, 'Yo, wuzzup.' And the girls are like, 'Ohhhh, Dallin. You're so awesome at football! We love you!' And I'm like, 'Heisman Trophy!'"

Awkward. Silence.

Outside, a tumbleweed rolled past the house.

"Still cheesed about the scrimmage, I take it."

Dallin put his sunglasses back on, for some reason. "You weren't at my scrimmage? I hadn't noticed."

"Really? Because you've been acting psycho ever since."

"Your face is acting psycho ever since."

"What?"

"Nothing."

The iPad on the nightstand beeped. "Hold that thought." Zoey grabbed the iPad. On-screen, a message blinked: *21 New Reservations.* She shook her head and giggled. Two days earlier, the developers in Kandahar had launched the Zoeylicious website. Customers could book reservations through a dedicated page. Already, Zoeylicious was booked out through September. (On a sadder note, the site did not smell or taste like chocolate chip cookies.)

"I rest my case," Dallin said.

It took Zoey a second to remember what they were talking about. "Dal, did your coach even play you?"

Dallin winced. Even with the sunglasses on, Zoey saw it. He wandered over to the Wall of Fame. Not to read the reviews, Zoey suspected, but for an excuse to turn his back to her.

"You still haven't said sorry," Dallin grumbled. "I noticed that."

Zoey was on her feet now, though she didn't remember

standing up. "That's why you came over? You want an apology?"

"You can't do it, can you?"

"What, apologize?"

"That's right."

"I can apologize."

Dallin spun to face her. "Let's hear it, then."

He stared at her.

She stared back.

"See?" Dallin said. "You can't do it."

"You want an apology? Fine. I'm sorry I'm so awesome that the New York Times practically kidnapped me to do an interview. Happy?"

Dallin put his hands into his pockets and looked up at the ceiling, like people do when they're waiting for an elevator and they don't wanna make chitchat with the other people waiting. "You can't admit you're wrong either."

"And they say girls like to make drama."

Dallin headed for the bedroom door.

"Where are you going?"

"Anywhere but here." He stopped in the doorway. "Just once, it'd be cool if my stuff was as important as your stuff. Just one time."

His words stung Zoey like jellyfish tentacles. *I don't need this*, Zoey thought. *I'm a critically acclaimed chef, not a punching bag. Speaking of which . . .*

"I'll see you tonight, right?"

"Sure." Dallin stepped into the hall, out of sight. "Unless someone asks me for an interview."

Uh-oh. Was that a threat? Was Dallin planning a

no-show tonight? He was Trolley 2's only server. Without him, Zoeylicious couldn't operate. She couldn't risk it.

"Wait!" She dashed into the hall, catching Dallin at the top of the stairs. "You look hungry. Are you hungry? I'll make you something big and delicious to eat. Anything you want. You say it, I'll make it."

Dallin brightened. "Anything?"

Heat

Two hours later, Zoey sent Dallin home with a tummy full of Bacon-and-Kit-Kats-Burgers and a smile on his face. As she transferred dishes and utensils from the table to the soapy sink, Gershwin strolled into the kitchen. "Hi-de-ho, Chef," he said, setting a plastic bag on the table.

"Whatcha got there?" Zoey said.

"The curiosity is killing me." Gershwin reached into the bag and pulled out a pair of latex gloves. "Grab the mayo, will ya?"

Zoey dropped a handful of knives into the sink. "You didn't."

"Wanna watch?"

"Of course."

Zoey searched the fridge for mayo while Gershwin, gloved up now, unpacked metal tongs and a bag of six orange-red peppers the size of Salinas strawberries.

Zoey set a jar of Trader Joe's Organic Mayonnaise on the table. Curious, she picked up the bag of peppers and sniffed inside. A sharp, piquant smell singed her nose hairs. She dropped the bag. "Want me to call an ambulance first?"

Gershwin held up the tongs and *clacked* the bits together. "Don't tell your mother." Grinning like a mad scientist, he inserted the tong's arms into the bag and fished out a single pepper. He inspected the vegetable like a jeweler inspects a fine gem. "You only live once," he said, and popped the pepper into his mouth.

He chewed.

And waited.

"Well?" Zoey said.

Her father sniffled. "It ain't bad. Sweet, in fact."

"Your nose is running."

Gershwin gripped the edge of the table. "Wait. Here it comes." His cheeks turned red. "Wow, this is . . ." He coughed. "This pepper doesn't mess around." Tears formed in his eyes. He pounded his palms on the table.

Zoey hadn't seen her dad in this much pain since the time he ate six unripe ackees and got Jamaican vomiting sickness. (Yes, that's a thing.) Or the time he tried to out-eat Dallin at a pizza buffet. Or the time he took up sword swallowing.

"Dad, you have a problem." She put down the cereal box and patted him on the back.

Gershwin coughed again. Sweat trailed down his forehead, and tears crawled down his cheeks. He dabbed his cheeks with his sleeve. "Holy guacamole, that stings."

Zoey twisted the lid off the jar of mayonnaise. "Here."

Chest heaving, Gershwin held the jar to his trembling mouth. He slurped and sucked as goopy mayo oozed down his chin. Swallowing, he set the jar on the table and wiped his chin with his palm. He smiled. "That was awesome. You should sell these in your restaurant."

"I wanna nourish my customers, Dad, not kill them." Zoey put the bag of peppers in her pocket. "It's for your own protection."

Gershwin rubbed his hands down his discolored face. "I feel . . ." He leaned to the left. Then more to the left. Then yikes-he's-about-to-fall-out-of-his-chair to the left.

"Yep, this is happening." Zoey sprang from her chair and helped Gershwin to his feet. "Really, should I call an ambulance?"

"I'll be fine. Help me upstairs to my room. I need a nap."

"We roll out in four hours."

"I'll be ready."

Zoey draped Gershwin's arm over her shoulders. Like a soldier rescuing a wounded comrade from the battlefield, she helped him upstairs.

At the top of the stairs, Gershwin dropped to his knees. "I'll lie down here."

"Dad, your bed is like ten steps away."

"Not worth it." He lay down on the floor, his feet hanging over the edge of the first step. He folded his arms under his face like a pillow, closed his eyes, and became still.

Zoey's phone rang in her bedroom. She checked her father's pulse to make sure he wasn't dead (he wasn't), then zipped into her room to answer it. Her phone was on the nightstand, next to the iPad. She checked the caller ID.

UNAVAILABLE.

Zoey never received calls from people she didn't know. Her number was unlisted and on the federal government's Do Not Call list (Valentine had insisted). Perhaps Knuckles was calling from a new burner phone. He changed phones every week, said it was "safer this way."

She answered. *"Oui?"*

"Yes, hello, is this Chef Zoey?"

"Who's asking?"

"My name is Faruq al-Falafel. I'm Royston Basil Boarhead's personal assistant."

Wham. Adrenaline rush.

"This is Chef Zoey. How may I be of service?"

"Your video on the *New York Times* website is making the rounds at *Golden Gate Magazine*. You've piqued Mr. Boarhead's curiosity. He wants me to eat at your restaurant tonight, get a feel for things, as it were. I tried to make a reservation online but you're booked out through September."

"A table just became available," Zoey said. "Six thirty, Jefferson and Hyde."

"I'll see you then. Goodb—"

"Wait. How did you get my number?"

"I asked Chef Cannoli. He didn't want to give it to me, said it was a matter of privacy. I had to beg. It wasn't pretty."

"I'm glad he caved. See you at six thirty, Mr. al-Falafel."

"Thank you."

Zoey traded her phone for her iPad. She logged into her site's reservations page. Every table at every time slot was booked. How was she supposed to fit Mr. al-Falafel in? There had to be a way.

She noticed something: a Tom Salado and a Wendy Pfeffer, each with a reservation for one at a table for two. Happy to play Cupid, Zoey changed their reservations to the same table. This way, Tom and Wendy would enjoy a romantic dining experience together, and there'd be a free table for Faruq al-Falafel. *Parfait.*

"Holy guacamole, I'm gonna cook for Royston Basil Boarhead's personal assistant!" The notion was exhilarating and terrifying and *I-can't-believe-this-is-happening*-ing. The iPad beeped.

Homescreen. 2 New Alerts.

@ChefZoey: You have 78 new subscribers. 3,993 total subscribers.

And:

BuzzShark Alert—Today, 9:58 a.m.
We detected your buzzword, Zoeylicious, trending <u>here</u>.

The <u>here</u> brought Zoey to the comments section beneath Eat Girl's blog post about Zoeylicious. (Reads: 7,805. Shares: 2,039.) Eat Girl was one of Zoey's favorite food bloggers, and she had posted a killer review of Zoey's cuisine earlier that week. The latest comment on her post was from one—*uh-oh*—@NewShanghai.

Zoey is bad chef. Zoey pet sick dog and no wash hand. Food taste like dead skunk. Make you sick. You no eat at Zoeylicious. Come to New Shanghai, we give you half off meal. New Shanghai food is delicious healthy. Better than pork chop.

Zoey was gripping the iPad so hard the screen almost cracked. *Oh no you didn't.* She swapped her iPad for her phone and dialed New Shanghai.

The hostess answered after one ring. "New Shanghai."

"Chef Pao. *Now.*"

"Who is calling?"

"The adorable and undeserving victim of his nefarious slander!"

"One moment, Zoey."

Zoey heard the phone change hands. Chef Pao came on the line. "*Nĭ hăo*, Chef."

"I read your comment, you cockroach! You're a liar and a villain!" Zoey lowered her voice to sound like a bad guy from the cop movies her dad liked to watch. "My dumplings got you pretty scared, didn't they?"

Chef Pao chuckled, sort of. The chuckle was slow, deep, and calculating. Between each "huh" lingered a second of ominous silence. "Me scared? No. You should be scared."

"I'm warning you, you better not write another word about me or I swear I'll—"

"Oh," Chef Pao said, "I plan to do much more than write about you."

Zoey didn't like the sound of that. It was vague and foreboding, like a hot sandwich named after an extinct animal. "What's that supposed to mean?"

She waited. No reply. "Hello? Yo, Pao, you there?"

Silence.

Zoey looked at her phone. *Call ended.* "Not. Cool." She kicked the air. She punched her bed. She felt bad because the bed had done nothing to deserve that.

Chef Pao's threat played and replayed inside her head: "Oh, I plan to do much more than write about you."

What, exactly, is Chef Pao planning?

An Unexpected Offer

On a yoga mat in her bedroom, dressed in a weightless silk *kamishimo*, Zoey sat in the lotus position, preparing her mind, body, and spirit for an evening of culinary zen.

The doorbell rang. Since Valentine was away and Gershwin was passed out at the top of the stairs, Zoey would have to deal with the visitor herself. Annoyed, she slogged downstairs and opened the front door.

Chef Cannoli stood on the stoop landing, dressed in pressed kitchen whites and leaning on his black cane. A white Fiat sat in the driveway, engine idling. Panzanella sat in the driver's seat, her flowing black hair draped over one shoulder.

Despite their long-standing professional relationship, this was the first time Chef Cannoli had visited Zoey's house.

"Everything okay?" Zoey said.

"Yes, is fine. Pardon me for visit without announcement."

"You're welcome anytime. Wanna come in?"

"No, *grazie*. I no can remain for long time." His thumb stroked the lion's head atop the cane as if it were a living animal. "Congratulations for your, em, many positive reviews. The things, they are moving fast for you."

"So far, so good."

Chef Cannoli's hand trembled, causing the cane to wobble. "*Sì*, is very good. *Bambina*, em, you know what thing tomorrow is?"

"Yeah. Sunday."

"You know what important *evento culinario* is to happen?"

"All-you-can-eat waffles day at IHOP?"

"Tomorrow morning, *Golden Gate Magazine* is to announce the three, em . . . what is word? *Candidati*."

Candidati wasn't part of Zoey's limited Italian vocabulary, but the word sounded like . . . "Sweet smoldering sauerkraut! That's tomorrow? I've been so busy, I totally forgot. Wait, do you have inside information? Will you be nominated? Will I be nominated? Am I cooking for Royston Basil Boarhead tomorrow? Is that why you're here?"

Chef Cannoli made an *easy-tiger* gesture with his free hand. "My sources at the magazine, they say I am to be nominated."

"Let me guess. Chef Pao . . . ?"

"Yes, nominated also."

"Who's the third candidate?"

"The magazine is yet deciding. Is between two chefs from India, I think."

"Oh." Zoey fought back a wave of jealousy. "Congratulations. You must be stoked."

Chef Cannoli did not look stoked, however. His brown eyes radiated gloom and worry, and his shoulders sagged like under-baked cupcakes. "Is *imperativo* I win tomorrow. It is to be *la mia ultima* chance."

"Your last chance? Why?"

Chef Cannoli sighed as if the question itself had zapped the last of his diminishing strength. "I'm old, Zoey. I walk with a cane. My back hurts always. My vision is blurry. Sometimes I no can read my own recipes. At the end of this year, I will retire myself. I must win the Golden Toque tomorrow or I never will. I want you to help me, Zoey. I want to hire you."

Zoey bit her lip to keep her jaw from dropping to the ground. Had Cannoli offered her the job a year earlier, she would've jumped at the opportunity. But now . . . "I'm not for hire, Chef. I own a restaurant, remember?"

"I'm not asking this of you to give up your restaurant. Only put on hold for a little time. Work at my restaurant tonight. I will train you in the ways of *mia cucina*. Tomorrow you will to be my sous chef."

"But you already have a sous chef. Chef Fellini has been your right-hand man for three years now."

"And for three years I have come in for the second place." Chef Cannoli's eyes darkened. "I have need for you, *bambina*. Together, you and I can bring Chef Pao to his knees."

"I don't know."

Chef Cannoli produced a check and handed it to Zoey. "This is your payment for one day and two nights of work."

When Zoey saw the amount on the check she almost fainted. "Whoa, this is . . ."

"A lot of money."

"You can say that again."

"A lot of money."

"That was a figure of speech."

"A lot of money?"

"No, 'You can say that again.' It means, 'You got that right.' You weren't supposed to actually say it again."

"You say to me to say it again. I say it again. Now you say I no supposed to say it again. What is point of this?"

"Forget it." Zoey's fingers twiddled the check. "I have to think about this."

"Think? What is to think? I pay to you much money. You work for me two nights. I win the Golden Toque. You open up again the Zoeylicious. Is simple."

Zoey had to admit, working for Chef Cannoli would be pretty cool, and the pay, for two nights' work, well, that was pretty cool too. But Zoeylicious . . .

"I have to think about this."

"I tell to you this thing: if you accept offer, you arrive to La Cucina before the six p.m. If you no show, I will to understand you no accept mine generous offer. Deal?"

"Sure."

With the aid of his cane, Chef Cannoli limped back to the Fiat idling on the driveway.

Zoey closed the door. Gershwin stood nearby, his arms folded, his complexion back to its regularly scheduled color. "How much is the check?"

"Dad, you were eavesdropping?"

"Yes. How much is the check?"

"You wouldn't believe me if I told you."

Gershwin took the check and looked it over. "Chef Cannoli doesn't mess around. Are you going to accept?"

"I don't know. It's a lot of money."

"Is that why you got into the restaurant business, for the money?"

"Well, no."

Gershwin folded the check in half. "I heard you talking on the phone. You said a table became available. Who were you talking to?"

"You were eavesdropping on my phone call too?"

"Yes. Who was it?"

"Do you listen in on every conversation I have in this house?"

"Yes. Who was it?"

"He was Royston Basil Boarhead's assistant. He wanted to visit the restaurant tonight."

Gershwin whistled the way men do when they see an expensive sports car. "*Golden Gate Magazine.* That's a big deal."

"Yeah."

"I saw the *New York Times* video. What was it the lady said about your pork chops?"

"World's greatest."

"High praise. I bet Boarhead's assistant is anxious to try them."

"He didn't mention them specifically."

"Chef Cannoli said *Golden Gate Mag* already chose two candidates for the Golden Toque. How many candidates will there be, total?"

"Three."

"So one spot is still available."

"Yeah."

"And Boarhead's assistant is vetting Zoeylicious tonight."

Zoey hadn't thought about that. Was that why Royston Basil Boarhead had told his assistant to eat at Zoeylicious this evening? Not soon, not next week sometime, but *tonight*? Nah, it couldn't be. Could it?

Gershwin bent down and kissed Zoey's cheek. "I'm sure you'll make the right decision. If you need me, I'll be in the kitchen sucking on a mayonnaise Popsicle."

Gershwin handed the folded check to Zoey and walked into the kitchen.

Zoey stared at the check.

She looked out the window at Zoeylicious, parked along the curb.

She stared at the check again.

You only live once.

She ripped the check in half and let the pieces fall to the floor.

Bugged

Zoeylicious arrived at Jefferson and Hyde at 6:30 p.m. A crowd of hungry customers filed into Trolleys 2 and 3. Dallin and Gershwin had to turn half of the people away. "Sorry. Reservations only."

A few parties pretended to have reservations. One man accused Gershwin of losing his party's reservation. Gershwin, who dealt with swindlers and fast-talkers on a regular basis (you know, jazz clubs), saw through the tactic and sent the man packing.

Dallin ushered Faruq al-Falafel to Table 1 and wished him a "happy dining experience." Then he stepped over to Table 2 to check on Tom Salado and Wendy Pfeffer.

"Tonight's meal is on the house," he told them. "If all goes well, please ask about Zoeylicious's wedding catering packages, perfect for your special day."

By 6:45, every reservation was accounted for, every table was occupied, and Zoeylicious was on the move. In Trolley 3, Valentine & the Night Owls riffed on a slow jam as cool as watermelon gazpacho. In Trolley 2, Dallin came to the serving windows. "Table one wants the S'meesecake."

"Roger that." Zoey rubbed her hands together. *Okay, Mr. al-Falafel, get ready for the best S'meesecake you've ever had.*

While Dallin tended to other tables, Zoey darted to the walk-in fridge. The walk-in door was so heavy she had to pull with both arms to get it open. She stepped inside and turned on the light. For a fraction of a second, she thought she saw the floor move. No, it must've been the swaying of the trolley and the sudden change from dark to light tricking her senses.

Zoey took a cheesecake from the pie rack. She paused. Something about the cheesecake looked . . . *wrong.*

She smelled it. *Smells fine.*

She scooped up a little bit with her pinkie, licked it. *Tastes fine.*

But something wasn't right. If only she could put her finger on—

At the center of the cake, the ivory filling bubbled up like a stalagmite.

"What the cheddar?"

A small black head burst out of the filling, gobs of cream dripping from its spindly antennas. Zoey recoiled with a shriek. The cheesecake hit the floor with a *splat!* The insect—a large cockroach—scampered for the shadows. Zoey stomped it with her boot, killing it dead.

She laid a hand on her pounding heart. *Stay calm, Chef. It was only a bug. And now it's dead. Sure, you don't know where it's been, or what it's touched, or if it had the black plague, and hundreds of creepy babies, and my once clean, health-code-compliant fridge is now a radioactive Ebola locker. HOLY CRUMPETS I'M GOING TO DIE!*

Her phone rang, making her jump. She checked the caller ID. *Gershwin.* She took a deep, steadying breath, and took the call. *"Oui?"*

"Hi-de-ho, Chef, I got two Caramel Popcorn Lasagnas, five Honey Nut Eggnogs, one Athens-Fried Cucumber Crab Gyro, and one S'meesecake."

"Got it."

Zoey put away her phone. She scooted the smushed cake aside with her boot. *Isolated incident. Stay in the game, Chef.*

Reaching for another cheesecake, she saw something move. Not on the cheesecake, but on a T-bone steak on a different shelf. A centipede, its creeping black legs tearing at the steak's raw flesh.

"Yuck city."

Zoey used a carrot to bat the centipede to the ground, then boom. Boot. Stomp. *Squish-squish.*

Something was very, very wrong. Ants, weevils—that's one thing. But a cockroach and centipede—that's horror-movie stuff.

The fridge crawled to life. Red ants swarmed in and out of bins of tomatoes, boysenberries, spinach leaves, and other produce. A furry gray tarantula slinked across a wheel of Brie cheese. Something long and green swam inside a jug of milk.

After throwing up in her mouth a little bit, Zoey fled the fridge. She flung her body against the massive door, heaving it closed. Her hands trembled. Her stomach writhed. *How did this happen?*

The top, bottom, and sides of the refrigerator door were flush with the stainless-steel frame. Airtight. Not even the tiniest specks of dusk could have squeezed through the cracks. So how'd the bugs get in?

Then it hit her. Like a hurricane.

I've been sabotaged.

She zoomed to the driver's box and flung open the door. "Knuckles, we got a problem!"

"What kinda problem?"

"A *big* problem. Last night—or this morning, or afternoon, I don't know when—Chef Pao snuck into my kitchen and bugged my ingredients!"

Knuckles pulled a lever, slowing the trolleys a little. "So let's stop at a grocery store, buy new ingredients."

"We can't *stop*. If we stop, people will think something's wrong. If they think something's wrong, they'll ask questions. If they ask questions, they'll find out my kitchen is infested. If they find out my kitchen is infested, they'll call the bogeyman—"

"Bogeyman?" Knuckles said.

"Health inspector."

"I get it. We gotta be discreet." Knuckles stroked his bushy black beard. "Hey, we could try the Montana '89."

"This is no time for dancing!"

"*Joe* Montana, 49ers QB, Super Bowl, 1989, threw the game-winning pass to John Taylor. Remember?"

"Wasn't born yet."

"Well, last summer, I was in San Quentin doing a stretch for . . . never mind what for. The warden was a real hardnose, wouldn't allow us basic amenities like Tabasco sauce and nunchakus. So we'd arrange for our girlfriends to meet us at the south fence at rec time. They'd quarterback over all kinds o' stuff: socks, pizzas, puppies, Xboxes, you name it. The guards never suspected a thing."

Zoey slapped Knuckles on the back. "Drive us to Beach Street. Hurry."

Zoey whipped out her phone and dialed a number she knew by heart, for she had dialed it hundreds of times. A man answered. "Hallo."

"Hey, Mr. Bregenwurst, it's me."

"Chef Zoey, how are you this fine evening?"

"In a pinch, actually. I need to place a huge order, and I need it ready in five minutes. Can you do that for me?"

"How big is the order?"

Zoey rattled off the names of various sugars, flours, marinades, herbs, spices, oils, cuts of steak, cuts of chicken, shrimps, lobsters, crabs, clams, salmons, sausages, pepperonis, fruits, vegetables, milks, creams, butters, cheeses, crackers, and chocolates.

Mr. Bregenwurst cleared his throat. "You need all this in five minutes?"

"Four minutes now."

"I'll see what I can do."

"How good is your throwing arm?"

"I beg your pardon?"

Zoey gave Mr. Bregenwurst the 411 on the Montana '89. "Only throw the groceries into Trolley One," she added. "Do not throw anything into Trolleys Two and Three or you'll hit my customers. Be inconspicuous. Tell your staff to draw as little attention to themselves as possible."

"Thirty-five years I've been in business," Mr. Bregenwurst said. "This is the strangest thing I've ever been asked to do."

"See you in three and a half minutes."

Dallin came to the serving window. "Table five wants the Mongolian Beef Lettuce Wraps with Celery Mushroom Chow Mein."

"It'll have to wait, Dal. I'm busy putting out a fire."

"Fire? Where?"

"It's a metaphorical fire."

"Oh." Dallin scratched his nose. "What's a meta . . . phim . . . orkal . . . ?"

"It means I'm dealing with a time-sensitive emergency that could, metaphorically speaking, burn my life to the ground. I need you to buy me some time. Go make small talk with the customers. Compliment the men. Flirt with the women. If you see a young couple, tell the girl she's lucky her boyfriend brought her to such a classy establishment. Keep them occupied so they don't notice the delay."

"Remind me what a 'metaphammer' is?"

"Go!"

Dallin approached a table of elderly Hispanic women. "You ladies look youthful this evening. Would you like to see my muscles?"

Zoey checked the rest of her kitchen for bugs and was relieved to not find any. With disinfectant rags, she wiped down every surface, every corner, every appliance. Twice.

As Zoeylicious turned onto Beach Street, Zoey opened all the windows on the right side of Trolley 1. She looked up the street and saw Bregenwurst Market. Men and women in green aprons were filing out its doors, hefting bulging grocery sacks.

Nearing the store, Knuckles slowed Zoeylicious to a

steady five-mile-per-hour crawl. And then the groceries started flying.

Zoey ducked behind the counter as dozens of grocery sacks sailed through the open windows, landing on counters, the sink, the stove, the floor. Next came items that didn't fit in grocery sacks: cured hams, racks of lamb, banana stalks, potato sacks, blocks of cheese, a four-pound bar of dark Ghirardelli chocolate.

By the time Trolley 1 had passed Bregenwurst Market, Zoey's kitchen had enough groceries to feed the 49ers defensive line. Zoey poked her head out the window and blew Mr. Bregenwurst a kiss. He tipped his hat and chuckled, bidding her *guten Abend.*

Zoey unpacked and organized the groceries, performed a quick mise en place, and set to work on the S'meesecake. She would have to make everything from scratch. Time was against her.

First, the crust. With a rolling pin, Zoey reduced a stack of graham crackers to a mound of rubble. She tossed the crumbs into a bowl, stirred in sugar, cinnamon, and soft butter. With her fingers, she spread the graham cracker goop onto the bottom and sides of a springform pan, creating a smooth, bowl-shaped crust. The crust looked so yummy that Zoey half considered serving it to Faruq "as is" and moving on to the next order.

On to the filling! In sixty seconds flat (a personal best), Zoey whipped flour, sugar, cream cheese, milk, and eggs into a cheesecake filling as smooth and fluffy as a whipped mousse. She scooped the filling into the graham cracker crust inside the springform pan.

Typically, a cheesecake takes an hour to bake. Zoey didn't have that kind of time. Fortunately, she knew a trick that would bake the cheesecake in three minutes or less. She hadn't tested the trick in years, but it had worked once, so it was worth a shot now.

Zoey fitted a lid onto the springform pan. She wrapped the pan in tinfoil. She placed that pan inside a bigger pan: a roasting pan. She poured boiling water into the roasting pan, submerging the bottom two-thirds of the springform pan. She fastened a lid to the roasting pan.

Using a wooden peel the size of a snow shovel, Zoey deposited the heavy roasting pan into the fires of the brick oven. If all went according to plan, the flames would heat the roasting pan, the roasting pan would heat the water, the water would heat the springform pan, and the springform pan would become a mighty super-oven, unbeholden to the laws of thermal dynamics. *Like Leonardo da Vinci but with food*, Zoey thought, remembering her first meeting with Miss Lemon.

Now, the s'mores.

Zoey unwrapped a one-pound bar of Ghirardelli dark chocolate. Under normal circumstances, she would have made the chocolate bar from scratch, but these weren't normal circumstances. She unwrapped the chocolate bar, set it on the block, took up her trusty, super-awesome Santoku, and chopped the bar into bits. Next, she unwrapped a dozen cubes of caramel, dropped them into a tin mug, and placed the mug on a hot burner. The caramel began to bubble and melt.

These tasks didn't quite occupy three minutes, but they

came close enough. With the wooden peel, Zoey retrieved the roasting pot from the brick oven.

Typically, a cheesecake needs four hours to chill and set. Again, Zoey would have to improvise.

Careful to not drop the red-hot roasting pan, she trekked across the kitchen. Holding the peel over the salt-water tank, she let the roasting pan slip off the blade into the cold water. Steam billowed from the top of the water. The pan *hiss*ed as it sank to the bottom of the tank. Zoey wondered if the ice-cold water would cool the pan in a hurry, or if the hot pan would cause the water to boil and cook all the crustaceans alive. To her relief, the cold oceanic water won the battle for dominance. The tank water didn't boil. The crustaceans stayed safe. The pan cooled in seconds.

Leaving the pan in the tank, Zoey impaled six jumbo marshmallows on a long roasting fork. She held the fork over the fire pit, six inches from the dancing flames. She waited until the marshmallows were golden brown and beginning to melt off the fork. (She didn't allow the marshmallows to catch fire. That would have created char. Zoey had a simple philosophy on char: great on pork, bad on marshmallows.)

Zoey set down the hot marshmallow fork, the handle on the counter, the middle of the fork leaned against a pan, the marshmallows hoisted in the air.

She reached into the chilly saltwater tank. The roasting pan's handles were cold to the touch. Her back ached as she drew out the heavy pan and placed it on the counter.

Let's see if this worked.

She removed the lid from the springform pan. The cheesecake filling looked settled and beautiful, smooth and creamy, firm but delicate.

Relieved, Zoey removed the sides of the pan. She spread the gooey, melty golden-brown marshmallows evenly over the cheesecake. She added the chopped chocolate bar, whipped cream, and a cherry. For the final touch, she poured the mug of hot caramel in a pencil-thin zigzag down the center of the cake.

À la perfection.

Zoey handed the S'meesecake to Dallin in Trolley 2. Dallin carried the cake to Faruq. Holding her breath, Zoey watched Faruq take his first bite.

Faruq chewed.

He swallowed.

He blinked.

He breathed.

He gave Zoey a thumbs-up.

Zoey's legs were shaking. The muscles in her arms and neck felt overworked and tired. Zoey lumbered into the pantry. Sitting on a barrel of flour, she enjoyed a hunk of Chocolate Mexicano: Dark, Cayenne Pepper. She drew a deep calming breath. She closed her eyes, focusing her thoughts on the task still at hand. A restaurant full of hungry customers awaited. She had taste buds to rock.

I'll deal with Chef Pao tomorrow.

Night Crawler

Something fell. It wasn't big or heavy, but it was loud. Outside, on the street.

Zoey awoke with a start, which is never a good way to do anything, especially something as unpleasant as waking up. The digital clock on her nightstand glowed green. 3:03 a.m.

Static electricity crackled between her pajamas and sheets as she rose to kneeling position on the bed. Parting two blinds slats with two fingers, she peered out the window into the foggy dark, to the opposite side of the street, where Zoeylicious was parked. The trolleys were mere silhouettes, untouched by the meager house lights on Francisco Street. Behind the trolleys, the steep, vine-covered hill looked like a sleeping dragon, its leafy scales fluttering in the invisible wind.

She couldn't see anything to account for the loud sound—a *BAHFFFF!* it had been—that had woken her up. Of course, things were so dark and foggy she couldn't see much of anything. For all she knew, the sound had come from another street, or from her own dreams.

She watched and waited, wanting to know for sure that her trolleys were safe.

Minutes passed. Nothing moved. Nothing happened. Zoey was about to turn away from the window, lie down, and go back to sleep.

But then she saw something move. A figure, dressed in dark clothes, crouched atop Trolley 1 like a giant tarantula. At least, she thought it was a figure and she thought it had moved. Might've been the leaves beyond the trolley. Might've been nothing.

She continued to watch and wait. Until, at length, the figure moved again. It rose to its full stature. From her vantage point, Zoey couldn't tell if the person was short or tall, fat or skinny.

Zoey yanked the lift cord, and the blinds shot up to the headrail. She slid open her window, placed her hands against the screen, and shouted, *"Freeze! FBI!"*

The prowler ran for it, leaping from the roof of Trolley 1 to the roof of Trolley 2, then from Trolley 2 to Trolley 3, then onto the street, landing with a roll. It raced toward Hyde Street, formless, like a living shadow, at once visible and invisible.

There was no point chasing the prowler. He or she or it had too big a head start. Besides, the prowler was probably armed and Zoey was in no mood to get murdered.

Turning onto Hyde Street, the prowler passed under a lamppost. While the light failed to reveal the person's face, it did expose one distinct feature:

A long braided ponytail, whipping in the wind like a violent snake.

The Short List

 The next morning, Zoey went to Mission Police Station. She found Officer Haggis in his windowless office, seated at a small desk, a raspberry Danish in one hand, a Styrofoam cup of black coffee in the other. The morning paper lay on his desktop, opened to the sports section.

"Good morning, Miss Kate. To what do I owe the pleasure?"

Zoey sat down onto a metal foldout chair next to a filing cabinet and rested her hands on her knees. "I've come to report a series of heinous crimes."

Officer Haggis set the Danish on a stack of folders on his desk. He wiped purple goo off his chin with his pinkie finger. "What are the crimes?"

"Slander, subterfuge, and sabotage."

"And the culprit?"

"A nefarious villain named Chef Pao. You must arrest him at once. He's at his restaurant right now. I'll wait here until you get back."

Officer Haggis sipped his coffee and scratched his

left eyebrow with the back of his free hand. "And how, exactly, did this guy commit slander, subterfuge, and sabotage?"

"He blogged wicked things about me. He bugged my pantry . . . *literally*. And last night he tried to break into my trolleys."

"Do you have proof it's him?"

"All you gotta do is look into his eyes. You'll see the darkness in his soul."

Officer Haggis set his cup on the desk and brushed buttery crumbs off his fingers. "I'm afraid the darkness of a man's soul isn't enough to press charges, Miss Kate. I need concrete evidence, something I can show a judge. Did you or anyone else see Chef Pao do these things?"

"No, but I can show you the comment he posted online. It's essentially a manifesto of his intent to sabotage me."

"I'm afraid an online comment isn't enough, Miss Kate. If no one saw Chef Pao commit an act of sabotage and you can't provide evidence, then I can't arrest him."

"In that case, we'll have to take matters into our own hands. Here's what I suggest." Zoey leaned forward and lowered her voice. "I'll go to my favorite Mexican eatery, where I'll enjoy a lavish lunch of pulled pork enchiladas and fried ice cream. I'm there all the time, so it's the perfect alibi. Meanwhile, you and your fellow officers will head over to New Shanghai. You'll lure Chef Pao outside, then stuff him into the trunk of your car. You'll drive Chef Pao out to the middle of nowhere and leave him there. When you're done, you'll send me a text that says 'The stroganoff is ready to serve.' Then I'll know that Chef Pao is out of the way. For a few days, at least. Any questions?"

170

Officer Haggis picked up his Danish and took a bite. As he chewed, he stared at a map of San Francisco taped to the wall. The silence bothered Zoey. Why wasn't he saying anything? Maybe he didn't like a part of the plan.

"If you don't like the stroganoff idea," Zoey said, "we can use other dishes. Potato salad. Homemade chili. Alder-planked salmon. Any food will do."

Officer Haggis swallowed and looked at Zoey. "Miss Kate, for the next sixty seconds, I'm going to sit in this chair and enjoy the rest of my coffee and Danish. When I'm done, if you're not out of this police station and on your way home, I'll call your parents. I wonder how they'd react to news that their only daughter is under arrest for attempting to recruit a law enforcement official to aid her in a kidnapping."

"Since Chef Pao is an adult, is it still considered kidnapping?"

"Zoey, go home."

Moments later, Zoey was stomping up Vallejo Street, dodging men with briefcases, women with bulky purses, boys on skateboards, and girls on frozen yogurt. Her iPhone rang. Still walking, she took out her phone and looked at the caller ID. The number had a local area code, but Zoey didn't recogn—

Smack!

Zoey collided with something hard. Scents of tobacco and fermented soybeans attacked her nostrils. She stumbled backward, dropping her phone.

"Clumsy girl," said a cold, cruel voice.

Zoey's vision blurred. She shook her throbbing head. Her sight wobbled into focus on a face she had hoped to never see again.

Chef Pao.

His long black ponytail hung over his left shoulder, the bamboo and rat skull dangling at the end like charms on a witch's bracelet. He fixed his eyes—one jade, one a wandering colorless orb—on Zoey and grinned like a wolf about to pounce on a tiny rabbit. He held a grocery bag with a stalk of flowering Chinese chives hanging out of the top.

"This is surprise," he said. "How is restaurant?"

"It's awesome, no thanks to you."

With his free hand, Chef Pao stroked his shriveled left ear. "I no understand your meaning."

"You sabotaged me."

"What sabotage mean?"

"Don't play dumb, Pao. I know it was you."

Chef Pao made an *I'm-acting-aloof-and-harmless-now-but-you-and-I-both-know-I'm-evil-to-the-core* face. (If you've ever looked a cat in the eyes, you've seen it.) "You have proof?"

"No, but I will."

Chef Pao snorted. "In that case, I suggestion you be extra careful."

He strode past Zoey, bumping her—hard—with a meaty shoulder. "You keep out of way," he said, disappearing into pedestrian traffic.

On the sidewalk, Zoey's cell phone rang again. She picked it up, checked the caller ID. Same number. Curious, she answered. "*Oui?*"

"Chef Zoey," said a voice as deep and thick as brown gravy, "this is Boarhead, editor in chief at *Golden Gate Magazine*."

Zoey froze.

Her hero. On the phone. Speaking directly to her. *Holy guacamole.*

"Hello, sir. To what do I owe the honor?"

"You made quite the impression on Faruq. He's been talking about you all morning. He swears your restaurant is the best in town."

"I'm flattered, sir." She suspected good news was coming, but she was anxious nonetheless.

"I trust Faruq's recommendations above all others. Besides my own, of course." Boarhead chuckled, amused by his own quip.

Zoey chuckled too. She didn't know a lot about men, but she knew this much: if you want to get on a man's good side, stroke the ego.

"At Faruq's urging, I am nominating you as a candidate for the Golden Toque."

Zoey couldn't believe it. She was so excited she wanted to throw her arms in the air, shriek with glee, and dance the hokey pokey. But she remembered something Dallin had told her once: "When you get to the end zone, act like you've been there before." Zoey didn't know what an "end zone" was, but Dallin had explained, "When you do something awesome, don't act surprised. Act like, 'Oh, was that awesome? I hadn't noticed. I do awesome so often I forget to be amazed sometimes.'"

Zoey played it cool. "I'm honored, sir."

"As you should be," Boarhead said. "Your competitors are Chef Cannoli and Chef Pao. Are you familiar with their work?"

At the mention of Chef Pao, Zoey gritted her teeth. "Oh, I'm familiar with it."

"This afternoon, I shall dine at Chef Cannoli's restaurant. At six o'clock, I shall dine at Chef Pao's restaurant. At nine o'clock, I shall dine at your restaurant."

"I'll save you a table, sir. At nine o'clock, we'll be at Polk and Pacific. Can you meet us there?"

"I can."

"Great. I look forward to—"

"I expect great things from you, Chef. Do not disappoint me."

"I won't, sir."

"At nine, then."

Click.

Zoey looked up at the sky, her heart a storm of conflicting emotions. On the one hand, she was excited to cook for her hero. On the other hand, she was nervous. She was anxious to crush Chef Pao. Try to, at least. But if she crushed Chef Cannoli too, what would happen to their friendship?

The stakes were high, as were the chances of Chef Pao attempting another sabotage. Zoey would have to take preventative measures.

She dialed Knuckles. He answered, "Yeah."

"Knuckles, it's me. I want you to spend all day in the trolleys, keep an eye out for Chef Pao. Got it?"

"I don't wanna spend all day in the trolleys."

"Too bad. As chief executive of restaurant security, it's your duty to guard the trolleys today."

"Since when am I the chief executive of restaurant security?"

"Since twenty seconds ago. I just promoted you."

"Pay raise?"

"No."

Knuckles grumbled. "I'll head over."

Zoey ended the call then dialed Chef Cannoli. He answered. *"Buongiorno."*

"Hey, it's me."

"Zoey Kate, my dear *bambina. Come stai?*"

"I'm fantastic! You've heard the news, I assume?"

A pause. "News?"

"Royston Basil Boarhead nominated me for the Golden Toque."

A long pause. Then, *"Congratulazioni."*

"Thanks. Heads up. Last night, Chef Pao sabotaged my restaurant. Odds are he'll try again tonight. I suspect you're a target too. Be on guard."

Chef Cannoli gave a quiet grunt, the kind elderly people make when sitting down. "Why have you to warn me? You no want the award to win?"

"Of course I wanna win, but I wanna win because Royston Basil Boarhead loves my cooking, not because Chef Pao tipped the scales. Besides, you're my friend. I don't want anything bad to happen to you."

"Grazie, Zoey. I'll keep the eye out for Chef Pao and his plays afoul. *Buona fortuna* tonight. May the best chef win."

"May the best chef win," Zoey said.

Trouble, Part 1

Royston Basil Boarhead looked bigger in pictures than he did in real life. He stood on the corner of Polk and Pacific, next to an arthritic old woman who was taller than he was. As Chef Zoey stepped off Trolley 1 to shake his tiny hand, she found herself looking down at him. The only things big about Boarhead were his handlebar mustache and the gold watch chain on his wool vest.

"Thank you for coming, sir. It will be my honor to cook for you."

Boarhead brushed an invisible fleck of dust off one shoulder of his wool suit. "Yes, it will be."

Zoey wanted to ask him about his experiences at La Cucina di Cannoli and New Shanghai, but she worried such an inquiry would be inappropriate. So she said, "I hope you saved room."

Boarhead patted his pudgy belly. "I have a highly efficient digestive tract. There's always room. Which car is mine?"

"Trolley Two, *s'il vous plaît.*"

Boarhead brushed past Zoey (he smelled of hair wax and cherry mouthwash) and boarded Trolley 2. As Dallin ushered Boarhead to Table 1, Zoey hopped aboard Trolley 1. She gave the driver's box door a staccato two-knuckle knock, and the restaurant started forward. In Trolley 3, Valentine & the Night Owls eased into a smooth 9/8 waltz, and Valentine's sanguine trumpet floated over the rhythm section like steam over a boiling pot.

Washing her hands, Zoey was glad she didn't have to worry about Chef Pao interfering again. Knuckles had spent all day in the trolleys, keeping watch and searching for anything amiss. Having found "no signs of foul play," Knuckles was confident that the previous night's 3:00 a.m. break-in attempt had failed and the trolleys were in fine working order.

Dallin came to the serving windows. "Okay, Boarface wants the Choc Chops."

"And to drink?"

"He asked what I recommended. I said you had something special planned for him."

"Well done, Dal."

"Thanks. Oh, and the lady at table five requested Balsamic Pear Ravioli with Rose Petals. It's not on the menu. I told her I'd ask."

"Scoot."

Dallin stepped aside so Zoey could see Table 5. There she was, by herself, dressed in a mint-green executive skirt and blouse; Miss Lemon of Mulberry Bank.

Zoey said, "Did she sound calculating and vengeful or kind and gentle?"

Dallin said, "Um, kind and gentle, I guess."

"Did she say anything about pit bulls?"

"No."

"Okay. Tell her we're out of rose petals, but I got something even better planned. Something special, just for her. And if she tries to hand you a sealed envelope, don't take it. And it's Boarhead, not Boarface. If in doubt, use 'sir.'"

"Boarhead or sir. Got it."

In Trolley 1, a chain dangled from the ceiling. At the bottom of the chain, a metal hook. Attached to the hook, a tin drum.

Zoey lit a match and dropped it in the fire pit. *WHOOSH!* A massive blue-and-yellow flame shot up like a geyser, engulfing the bottom half of the suspended tin drum.

Zoey slid her hands into a pair of insulated leather gloves. She opened a hatch at the top of the tin drum. Heat rushed from the opening, stinging Zoey's face and arms. Taking care to not bump or graze the tin drum with any part of her body (even a split second of contact would've burned through her clothes and skin), she poured a sack of cacao beans into the drum and closed the hatch.

Gloves off, she fetched a brick of butter from the walk-in, unwrapped the brick, and plopped it into a hot saucepan on the stove. While the butter melted, Zoey sliced up six Pink Lady apples and tossed them into the pan.

The cacao beans in the tin drum began to *crackle* and *hiss* like popcorn. Gloves back on, Zoey unfastened the tin drum from the metal hook. She flipped the drum upside down, pouring a mess of husks and nibs onto the counter. She put the drum back on the hook, then shed her gloves.

The anvil was under the counter. It was heavy, but not so heavy that Zoey couldn't lift it. She raised the anvil over the pile of husks and nibs, and let it drop.

CRUNCH!

She moved the anvil aside. The husks were cracked and broken, but the rock-hard nibs—those opulent brown orbs of cacao—remained intact.

She took a blow-dryer from a drawer, plugged it in, set it to max, and aimed at the pile. The cracked husks winnowed away like sawdust. The weightier nibs stayed put.

Into the grinder went the nibs. The grinder rattled and hummed as it worked the nibs into cocoa liquor.

Dallin came to the window. "Yo, Chef, trouble at four."

Alarmed, Zoey bolted to the serving windows. At Table 4 sat two young men dressed in matching red tracksuits, their heads shaved to the skin. One guy had his legs propped up on the table. He was juggling a fork and butter knife high in the air, using grandiose gestures befitting a circus clown. The other guy pounded his fists on the table, chanting in Chinese, "*JIĀ-YÓU! JIĀ-YÓU!*"

"They're Chef Pao's men," Zoey told Dallin. "I recognize their faces." The messy, mostly empty plates and glasses on the table meant the men had already dined. "How long have they been acting like this?"

"Just started."

"That means they were waiting for Boarhead to arrive. That's Pao's plan: send in two jerks to cause a ruckus, ruin Boarhead's dining experience, make it impossible for him to enjoy himself, and impossible for me to win high marks."

The juggler bounced to his feet. He pranced up and down the aisle on his feet and knuckles like a monkey making threatening noises.

In a surprising (if not awkward) show of bravery, Royston Basil Boarhead rose to his feet, throwing a napkin to the floor for dramatic effect. "That's enough, gentlemen.

Either find your manners or find your way to the door."

The men were unfazed, and with reason. Zoey had seen bagels more intimidating than Boarhead.

Zoey said, "Dal, can you get rid of them?"

"Easy," Dallin said. "Unless they know kung fu."

The monkey guy performed a cartwheel and backflip, landing in a crouched position with one hand raised in a fist, the other bent like a monkey's paw. The second rose from the table and whipped off his red jacket, exposing two tattoos of green-and-yellow dragons on his cut chest and abs. With a mighty *"Hai!"* he jumped and flipped, kicking the air above his head. He landed legs apart, hands curled like claws.

Dallin gulped. "This one's above my pay grade, Z."

Zoey hollered to the driver's box, "Knuckles, crowd control!"

The restaurant screeched to a halt. Knuckles erupted from the driver's box with fire in his eyes. He titled his head to one side. The bones in his neck went *pop-pop-pop-pop!* like crushed Bubble Wrap.

"Time to take out the trash."

He hopped over to Trolley 2. When Miss Lemon saw him, she recoiled in fear, as did her fellow diners. Boarhead dropped to his knees and crawled under Table 1. Pao's men altered their battle poses. They flexed their muscles, breathing through flared nostrils and clenched teeth.

"I'll make this simple," Knuckles said. "You can walk outta here or fly outta here. Yer choice."

"Hai!" Monkey Guy lunged forward, leading with a bent knee and cross-elbow. He struck Knuckles in the chest and face. When Knuckles didn't budge, Monkey Guy

attacked him again. Knuckles stood there, absorbing the blows, looking bored and underwhelmed. After Monkey Guy had worn himself out a little, Knuckles said, "Nice try, bumpkin." He seized Monkey Guy by the seat of his pants and pitched him out the door, onto the street.

Miss Lemon fanned herself with a menu.

Now the second guy charged. With deft force, he leapt into the air, extending one leg and hissing like a dragon.

"That's cute," Knuckles said, catching the guy midair, grabbing the seat of his pants, and throwing him out on the street too.

The diners applauded. Someone shouted, "Dinner and a show!"

Boarhead crawled out from under the table and brushed off his knees. "Well, that was exciting, wasn't it?"

Miss Lemon marveled at the tattooed hero standing in the doorway, muscles bulging. She had a *now-that's-what-I-call-a-man!* look on her face. (If you've ever been to a Chef Curtis Stone book signing, you've seen it.)

As Knuckles turned to leave, Miss Lemon cried out, "Wait! You never told me your name."

Knuckles glanced back over his tattooed shoulder. "They call me . . . Chrome Justice."

Miss Lemon fainted.

A minute later, the trolleys were back in motion, Dallin was helping Miss Lemon off the floor, and Zoey was about to make Golden Toque history.

Trouble, Part 2

After that rejuvenating chapter break, Zoey poked the sautéed apples with a fork. Juice oozed from the apples' soft flesh. She added cornstarch, cold water, brown sugar, cranberries, and ground cinnamon to the pan, making the kitchen smell like cranberry apple pie.

While chemistry did its thing in the pan, Zoey checked the grinder. The nibs were now a smooth, velvety liquid. Zoey poured the liquor into a running conche machine. She added cocoa butter (imported from Holland), white cane sugar (from Madagascar), milk conche (from Stockton), two vanilla pods (from India), one cinnamon stick (from Brazil), and a dash of ground nutmeg (from Indonesia). She set the timer for five minutes (most conche machines took ten or more hours to create a smooth, balanced chocolate texture, but Zoey had calibrated her conche to do the job in a fraction of the time).

Still mindful of the Cranberry Apple Sauté, Zoey gave the pan a quick stir-toss.

Dallin came to the windows. "How're those chops coming?"

"Almost ready. Have other customers ordered yet?"

"Nah. Their heads are still spinning from the fight."

"Perfect."

For the drink, she poured a bag of ice cubes and three club sodas into a blender. Running the blender on low speed, she added a pound of chopped cucumbers, one lime (peel and all), a fistful of mint leaves, and a half cup of Indian sugar. She fitted a lid on the blender, ran the blades on high for fifteen seconds, then poured the frothy green contents into a tall glass.

She set a plate on the counter. She placed a scoop of gooey Cranberry Apple Sauté at the center of the plate. Next, Zoey opened the smoker. Savory smells of charred pork and apple wood chips caressed her nostrils. Reaching into the smoker, she withdrew a double rack of tender pork (in the smoker since noon). Juices dripped from the dark pink meat. Steam whirled from the ashy spinal column and rib bones.

Zoey plopped the double rack onto the cutting board. With her wicked-awesome Santoku, she whacked off two pork chops. She stacked these pork chops atop the cranberry apple bed on the plate.

The timer on the conche *dinged*. Zoey opened the machine, dipped her pinkie in the chocolate sauce, and licked her fingertip. *Silky. Creamy. Delectable.* She ladled the chocolate sauce onto the pork chops, smothering them enchilada-style.

As a final touch, Zoey placed a jumbo marshmallow atop each stack of chocolate-covered pork chops. The bottom half of each marshmallow melted into goo. The top half remained firm and flat. On this flat top she placed a mint leaf. This mint would serve as a palatal bridge between entrée and beverage.

Zoey allowed herself three seconds to marvel at her work. If the meal tasted as toothsome as it looked (Zoey was certain it did), then the Golden Toque was as good as won.

With the plates and drinks on a silver platter, Zoey waited for Zoeylicious to stop at a red light, then hopped over to Trolley 2. Chin up, shoulders back, Zoey approached the judge's table.

Boarhead laid his napkin on his lap. "Ah, here it comes."

The trolley made a fast, sharp left turn. The momentum pushed Zoey forward. She stumbled. Her fingers lost their grip on the platter. She dropped to one knee. She reached out. Her fingers caught the platter, saving the plate and drink, preventing what could have been a disastrous spill.

Boarhead plucked a pen and notepad from his breast pocket. "Close call," he said, poising to write. "How many spills do you see on a given night?"

"None." Zoey regained her feet. "Usually the starts and stops are as smooth as applesauce."

Zoey served Royston Basil Boarhead his Chocolate-Covered Pork Chops and Cucumber Lime Delight, then tucked the platter under one arm. "Thank you for this opportunity, sir. *Bon appétit.*"

Boarhead smelled his dish. He made an *Mmmmm* face. (If you've ever bitten into a hot, fluffy Krispy Kreme donut, you've made that face too.) With his fork and knife, he sawed off a piece of goopy pork chop. He set down the knife. He switched the fork from his left hand to his right.

He stabbed the tender, juicy meat. Chocolate dripped onto the plate as he raised the fork to his mouth. Careful not to soil his immaculate mustache, he placed the forked tines in his mouth. He closed his lips and withdrew the fork. The tines emerged shiny and clean.

He chewed, eyes fixed on his plate. In time, he swallowed. He peered through the serving windows into Trolley 1. Then he looked at Zoey. His face emanated awe and wonder. "Who else is in the kitchen?"

"Just *moi.*"

"Who taught you to cook like this?"

"I taught myself."

"You have no formal training?"

"I wanted to develop my own style. I never saw how that was possible if someone else was teaching me."

Gobsmacked, Boarhead sipped his Cucumber Lime Delight. Setting down the glass, he stared at his plate again. He treated himself to another hearty, chocolatey bite of pork chop. "You're a prodigy, like Mozart. I should write that down."

Zoey watched Boarhead doodle on his notepad. She wanted to say something gracious like "You're too kind" or *"Merci beaucoup,"* but no words came out. She was so overwhelmingly happy—so dizzy with glee—she couldn't even form a coherent sardine. (See? Nothing.)

The floor shook like a jackhammer. The chandeliers whipped back and forth like punching bags. Plates and utensils skidded off of tables. Boarhead clutched his table. Zoey clasped his plate and drink so they wouldn't spill. In Trolley 3, the band hit a sour note and stopped playing.

"It's an earthquake!" someone shouted.

The shaking stopped.

Boarhead tidied his slick mustache. "What in the name of P.F. Chang was that?"

"I beg your pardon," Zoey said. "I'll have a word with the driver."

Before Zoey could step away, Zoeylicious made a fast, hard left turn. Zoey flew forward, landing facedown on the judge's table. She heard gasps. She felt hot, sticky gooeyness in her eyes and on her cheeks and stomach. She felt hands grab her arms and lift her off the table, back onto her feet.

Zoey wiped bits of pork and cranberry from her stinging eyes and surveyed the judge's table. Both dinners were ruined, the plates cracked in half, the drinks overturned. Cucumber Lime Delight sloshed off the table onto Boarhead's lap.

Zoey wiped a tear from her apple-smeared cheek. "I'm so sorry. I'll make you new dishes."

As Dallin rushed to Boarhead's table to clean up the mess, Zoey jumped over to Trolley 1. Devastated and furious, she sprinted to the driver's box and jerked open the door.

"You cost me the Golden Toque, you maniac! Why'd you take that corner so fast?"

Knuckles's face was paler than pad thai rice noodles. Sweat dripped from his bare arms and hands. "Sumthin's wrong wi' the trolleys, Chef."

Only then did Zoey notice the trolleys were moving faster than usual. Much faster.

"Knuckles, slow down."

"Can't. Gears 'r jammed. Brakes ain't workin'. Look." Knuckles joggled a series of levers. Nothing happened. "I can't stop! I can't even slow down!"

Zoeylicious ran a red light. Cars honked and swerved to avoid collision. A yellow taxi crashed into a fire hydrant, and water exploded into the air.

Zoey swallowed the lump in her throat. "How did this happen?"

"Dunno," Knuckles said. "Everythin' worked fine last night."

"Can you fix it?"

"If I coulda, I woulda. Ya have t' get t' the emergency brake in Three, otherwise we'll all be . . ." Knuckles's jaw dropped. " . . . Uh-oh."

Zoey peered ahead and saw the cause for Knuckles's "Uh-oh."

Zoeylicious was careening down Lombard Street toward Russian Hill, the steepest, twistiest stretch of road in San Francisco. Parallel rows of towering town houses created a sort of urban canyon, down the middle of which the road snaked back and forth at thirty-degree angles, like switchbacks on a mountain trail. Pedestrians walked up and down stairways on both sides of the road, posing for selfies and discussing the city planner's chemical imbalance.

Knuckles gripped the steering wheel at nine and six. "Hold on tight, Zoey. There's only one way to do this."

Zoey pressed her palms against the insides of the doorway, bracing herself. Zoeylicious hit the Russian Hill ridge and went airborne. Screams of terror erupted from Trolleys 2 and 3. Zoeylicious landed half on the road, half on the flower beds between the switchbacks, sparks spewing from the undercarriages.

The trolleys barreled down the lane like a wrecking ball, smashing through curbs, trees and lampposts. Debris flew in every direction, pelting row houses, denting doors and smashing windows. Pedestrians scattered like ants in a flood, taking refuge in doorways.

Zoeylicious arrived at the bottom of Russian Hill, colliding with a yellow Volkswagen bus on the cross street. The bus spun away like a boomerang, its front smashed, its bumper ripped to pieces. Zoey wondered if the people inside the bus were okay. She doubted it. The hit was so fast and so hard, she'd be relieved to hear the passengers were still alive.

Lombard Street became straight again, but was still quite steep.

Knuckles swiped his palm over his bald scalp, raking back a helmet of hot sweat. "Emergency brake, Chef. Go!"

Heart racing, Zoey raced to the back of Trolley 1 and flung open the door. It flew off its hinges, grazed Zoey's head and crashed into the stove behind her. Stepping into the doorway, the rushing wind slapped the toque off her head. Her cheesecake-colored hair whipped her face like a flag in a storm. Four feet below, the street blurred past at eighty miles per hour. The wheels spat sparks and black smoke, and a metallic burning smell pricked Zoey's nose.

Across the gap, Trolley 2's door swung open and shut, open and shut.

Zoey readied herself in the doorway. Left foot back. Right foot forward.

Open and shut.

On the balls of her feet now.

Open.

She leapt. Trolley 2 consumed her like a swooping hawk.

Closed.

On her hands and knees, Zoey gazed with horror upon overturned tables, broken chairs, rolling plates, and shattered glasses. Frightened customers clung to tables, walls, and each other.

Dallin was in the corner, arms raised like a boxer, legs in a kung fu stance. A plate came flying toward him like a Frisbee. He made no effort to deflect the plate. It smacked him in the chest and broke into pieces. Then he shrieked like a ninja—*"WAH-aaaah-AHHH!"*—and jump-kicked the air, accomplishing nothing but looking proud of himself anyway.

On her feet again, Zoey hurtled across Trolley 2, dodging sliding chairs and spinning tables. Passing Boarhead (he was under the table again, this time in the fetal position), she remarked, "I hope this doesn't negatively affect your evaluation of my restaurant."

Zoey jumped over to Trolley 3, landing on her hands and knees again. The scene in Trolley 3 was as bad as the scene in 2.

Monk's upright piano had tipped over, keys down, broken wires protruding from its open top.

Bird was huddled in a corner, hugging his saxophone, saying, "Don't be scared, darling. I won't let anything bad happen to you."

Gershwin was in the same corner, clutching Zoey's mom, who was clutching her trumpet.

Four was in another corner, comforting two frightened

young women and doing his darnedest to not look so happy about it.

Fat Jo was seated at his drum kit, his calves and knees pressed against the sides of his kick drum, his left hand holding the hi-hat, his right holding the floor tom, his massive belly and chest securing the snare and hi-tom, his teeth clenched on the crash cymbal. Like a mama bear protecting her cubs.

Gershwin called out to Zoey, "What the sassafras is going on?"

"The brake!" Zoey answered, regaining her feet and running for the emergency-brake room in the rear corner.

She got to the door, grasped the doorknob, and turned.

At least, she *tried* to turn it. It wouldn't budge. Not even a little.

She shook the doorknob. Jiggled it. Pulled it.

It wouldn't turn.

She tried kicking the door while working the knob with both hands.

Nuthin'.

Gershwin came to her side. "Zoey, what are you doing?"

"On the other side of this door is the emergency brake."

"Is that what the lever thing is? I was looking at it last night, wondering."

"Wait, last night you were able to open this door?"

"I don't think it has a lock. Look, no keyhole."

Zoey inspected the brass doorknob. It was round and smooth. Gershwin was right. No keyhole. The door wasn't made to lock. So why wouldn't it open?

The speeding trolleys made an abrupt lane change,

sending Fat Jo and his drum kit tumbling to the ground. The crash cymbal landed on its side and rolled toward Zoey like a spinning blade. Zoey dove out of its way. Grazing the soles of her boots, the cymbal lodged itself in the wall like a swung ax.

The restaurant continued to gain speed. Cars honked and swerved. Dogs barked. Pedestrians shrieked. *How long is Lombard Street, anyway?*

Zoey rose up and stuck her head out the window. Two-, three-, and four-story row houses lined both sides of the street. At the end of this alley, some three hundred yards ahead, the street crooked right, a hard right, a turn the trolleys could not and would not make. As far as Zoeylicious was concerned, this turn was the end of the road. And beyond that end?

A thousand-foot drop.

And at the bottom of that drop? A private residential drive winding between the sheer, rocky cliff and a luxury condo complex. In other words: concrete.

Things were about to get real.

Back in Trolley 3, Monk, the fittest dude in Valentine & the Night Owls, was ramming the door with his meaty shoulder. He gave the door a royal beating, but the door still did not budge.

"We'll get more power with our legs," Zoey said. "We kick on three. Ready? One. Two. *Three.*"

Gershwin and Monk delivered a mighty kick, with simultaneous impact, but the door stayed shut.

"Again!" Gershwin said. "One. Two . . ."

As Monk raised his leg to kick the door, Zoeylicious hit a bump in the road, knocking him off-balance. He fell backward, cuffing the back of his head on the rim of Fat Jo's kick drum.

"Sweet Duke Ellington, that smarts!" he cried, wincing, his hands clutching his cranium, blood seeping through the cracks between his musical fingers.

Zoey looked out the window. Thirty seconds, maybe less, before Zoeylicious would reach the cliff. "We're dead meat!"

"Not yet, we're not!" Dallin Caraway appeared at the head of Trolley 3, his chest puffed out, his arms flexed. "Make way for Hurricane Dallin."

"No way!" Zoey said. "Monk couldn't do it, and he's three times your size. Let someone else try."

"Shhhh. I got this." Dallin bent his knees, stooped forward, and parked three fingers on the ground.

Twenty-five seconds until the cliff.

"Help me," Monk said, too dizzy to crawl out of the way.

Zoey and Gershwin helped Monk scoot aside, clearing a path between Dallin and the emergency-brake-room door.

Twenty seconds.

Zoey screamed, "Hurry, Dal!"

Dallin's eyes focused on the door. He snarled and gritted his teeth. "You are a machine. You are unstoppable like a train. Your bones are rock. Your blood is fire."

He appeared to be reciting a Gatorade commercial.

Fifteen seconds.

"DAL, WHAT ARE YOU WAITING FOR?"

Dallin placed one foot behind the other, his heels raised. "You are a force of nature. You've trained for this. You were born for this. This is your moment of glory. Take it."

Ten seconds.

Zoey shouted, *"GO, DAL!"*

Fat Jo, who sat on the floor holding his snare drum on his lap, called out, "Hut, hut, hike!"

Dallin charged toward the door, screaming like a warrior entering a fierce battle. He flung his whole body at the door. It burst off the hinges in an explosion of wood and metal. Dallin landed facedown on the floor, next to the emergency brake. He didn't move.

Eight seconds.

Lurching over shards of timber and metal—and Dallin—Zoey entered the tiny room. She clenched the lever with both hands.

Five seconds.

With all her might, she pulled the lever. A shrill, grinding *SCREEEEEEEEECH* sounded below her feet. The floor rumbled. Sparks shot from the undercarriage like fireworks. The trolleys shrieked to a halt.

Everyone in Trolley 3 lurched forward, landing on tables and dishes and each other.

Zoey rose to her knees and shook Dallin. "Dal, are you all right?"

Dallin's eyes were closed. He didn't move.

Zoey shook him harder. "Dal, wake up!"

Dallin's eyes opened halfway. He coughed. "Are we dead, Z?"

"No, Dal. We're alive. Everyone's alive thanks to you."

Dallin's chest heaved. "I wish my coach had seen that."

"He can't say you don't hit hard enough."

Dallin closed his eyes. "I'm a hurricane."

"Can you sit up?"

"No, I think I'll . . ." Dallin coughed. ". . . lay here . . . a while."

"Don't die before help gets here, 'kay?"

Dallin cleared his throat. It sounded like a clogged garbage disposal burping up scraps of lettuce and corn. "Ix-nay on the ie-day."

Zoey rose to her feet. She felt foggy, like a cloud had moved into the space between her brain and her eyeballs. Bits of wood and dust clung to the smears of gooey, sticky chocolate on her sleeves and the front of her jacket and skirt. She looked like she'd stepped on a land mine in a cocoa field. Felt like it too.

Through the windows she saw Boarhead stumbling out of Trolley 2. The ends of his handlebar mustache were lopsided. One end curved upward up like an antler. The other end sagged like an elephant's trunk. His clothes were as tattered and filthy as Zoey's.

"You stupid girl!" Boarhead shook his fists at her. "You could have killed us all! You're a menace to society! Your restaurant belongs in a scrapyard, and you belong in prison!"

Gershwin rushed to Zoey's side, stuck his head out the window. "Yo, Mustache! You throw one more insult at my daughter, I come out swinging. Got it?"

Outside, Boarhead tugged on the bottom of his suit jacket, as if it would somehow serve to fix his spoiled appearance and restore his dignity. "My readers will hear about this." He stomped off into the night.

Gershwin brought his head inside the trolley. Turning, he laid his hands on Zoey's shoulders, looked her in the eyes. "Are you injured?"

"No."

"In pain?"

"No." She was numb, in fact.

As Gershwin dashed over to Valentine, Zoey scanned Trolley 3—a wasteland of busted furniture, dishes, and instruments. Everyone looked frail and traumatized. (Except Four. He was still grinning like an idiot, those two trembling women clinging to his shirt.) Bird was on his knees, helping Monk sit upright. Monk blinked, slow and hard, like his eyes couldn't focus. Dallin was still on the floor where he'd landed. His eyes were closed like he was in a coma or something. At least he was breathing. Valentine sat on the floor, legs straight, back against the wall, her fingers caressing the dents in her beloved trumpet. She looked up and her eyes met Zoey's. The look on her face said it all:

You just had to start a restaurant, didn't you?

A Loud Quiet

 2:00 a.m. Saint Francis Memorial Hospital. Room 304.

Dallin lay on a hospital bed, his body draped in sterile white sheets. His eyes were closed. His chest rose and fell with each slow, silent breath. A gruesome lump of bumpy, knotty flesh sat on his forehead. The doctor had called it a "goose egg." Zoey thought "goose egg" was a misnomer. She had worked with goose eggs before. (Goose Egg Omelets, Goose Egg French Toast, Goose Egg Streusel . . .) Goose eggs were smooth and round and pretty. They did not look like that *thing* growing out of Dallin's forehead.

Dallin had suffered a concussion. The doctor, bless her heart, had spent fifteen minutes explaining to Zoey the difference between a concussion and a coma. "A coma," she had said, "is a state of deep unconsciousness lasting for an indefinite period of time. A concussion is *temporary* unconsciousness caused by a blow to the head. In twenty-four hours, Dallin should be as good as new."

The armchair was comfortable. Zoey was grateful for that. Just because her soul was in anguish didn't mean her body had to be. She sat beside Dallin's bed, watching him sleep, listening to the sporadic beeps of a brain-monitoring machine on the other side of the bed.

The lights were off. Muted moonlight seeped through an open window, giving texture to the darkness, accentuating straight lines and hard edges and that volcano on her best friend's face. Zoey could have turned the lights on, but she didn't. The darkness was comforting for some reason.

"Fumble," Dallin mumbled. (He talked in his sleep, like Gershwin.)

Valentine and Gershwin were in the hallway. The door was closed, but Zoey could hear their voices.

"I've called her cell six times," Valentine was saying. "She's not answering."

Gershwin said, "What's the name of the diner she works at?"

"I'll recognize it if I hear it."

"Orphan Andy's."

"No."

"Sharky's."

"No. It's an L word, I think."

"Lori's?"

"No."

"Lucky Penny?"

"No. What was the first one you said?"

"Orphan Andy's."

"I keep thinking of a tree for some reason."

"Pinecrest?"

"That's it."

Silence. "Bad number," Gershwin said.

"What number did you call?"

"The one on Pinecrest's site."

"Did you dial it in right?"

"I didn't dial anything. I pressed the link. It started ringing."

"Try dialing instead."

"How is that different?"

"Maybe the link is bad."

Silence. Then, "See? Bad number."

"Try SFoodie. Maybe it lists a different number."

"Why would SFoodie have the correct number and the official site have a bad number?"

"Hand me the keys."

"You're in no condition to drive. Look at your hands, Val. They're shaking."

"We can't *not* tell her. Her son has a concussion, for the love of Louis!"

"Shh! You'll wake Zoey."

"Ms. Caraway has to know."

"Fine, but I'm driving."

"What about Zoey?"

"We'll be back before she wakes up."

Footsteps started down the hall. They disappeared into an elevator with squeaky doors.

Zoey propped her feet up on the bed, crossed her ankles, and clicked the heels of her boots together. "Your mom's gonna blame *me* for this, you know."

Dallin's chest moved up . . . and down . . . up . . . and down . . .

"She's scary when she's mad," Zoey added. "I should leave the country."

. . . down . . . and up . . . down . . . and up . . .

"The doc's gonna do a lobotomy," Zoey said. "I told him, 'While you're in there, why not swap out his brain for a monkey brain?' If you wake up craving bananas, that's why."

. . . down . . . and up . . .

Zoey chuckled, not in response to anything funny, but in response to the anguish eating her soul. Laughter felt and sounded absurd and inappropriate, and yet, for that same reason, it felt and sounded *so darn good*.

. . . down . . . and up . . . down . . .

. . . still down . . .

Waiting for up.

. . . still no up . . .

The brain-activity machine began beeping, loud and fast.

"Dal . . . ?"

Beep. Beep. Beep. Beep.

She slid her feet off the bed and sat upright. "You okay, buddy?"

Beep. Beep. Beep. Beep.

She shook his arm. No response.

The beeps grew louder, more staccato. *Bee-bee-bee-bee-bee.*

Panicked seized her. *Is he dying? Is he dead?* She had to do something. Quick.

So she jabbed her finger in his eye.

"Dude!" Dallin awoke with a start. He clapped both hands over his right eye. "What is your problem?"

"I thought you were dead."

"So you stabbed my eye?" Dallin removed his hands from his face, blinked a dozen times. "Agh! I'm blind!"

"Settle down, Head Injury. The lights are off."

"Why are the lights off?

"To help you sleep, dummy."

"Was stabbing my eye supposed to help me sleep?"

The door opened. Hall light poured into the room. A nurse hurried in. He checked the brain-activity machine. He pressed a button, and the beeping stopped. "Is something wrong with your eye?"

Dallin pointed an accusing finger at Zoey. "She stabbed me."

The nurse looked at Zoey, concerned.

Zoey moved a finger in a circular motion around her ear: the international *he's-crazy* sign. She mouthed the word "concussion."

The brain-activity machine beeped.

The nurse patted Dallin on the shoulder. "Can I bring you a Pepsi or some cookies?"

"Nah," Dallin said.

Zoey was so shocked to hear Dallin turn down a sugary snack that she almost fainted.

The nurse left the room and closed the door. Darkness surrounded Zoey like a heavy blanket, making her feel snug and safe.

Dallin closed his eyes. "I'm going back to sleep. Keep your fingers out of my eyes, will ya?"

"Of course. Sweet dreams."

She watched his breathing slow down . . . and up . . . down . . . and up . . .

She tried to take comfort in Dallin's *still-alive*ness. She told herself everything was fine. (Not with her career, of course. That was a disaster. But with Dallin.) She was *here*, wasn't she? This counted, right? This made up for . . . things . . . right?

"Wanna talk?"

"No."

"Tell me about your scrimmage."

"You didn't come. Coach didn't play me. We lost by fourteen. Can I go to sleep now?"

"Sure."

Dallin rolled onto his side, turning his broad back to Zoey. *Let him rest,* Zoey told herself. *Let* it *rest.*

But she couldn't let it rest. That feeling, deep in her guts, was too . . . loud. Was that the word? No, not loud. It was like an itch on your back that moves when you try to scratch it. But deeper. Beneath the skin.

"Hey, remember when you got locked out of your apartment, so I came over and you boosted me onto the fire escape, and I climbed through the window and let you in?"

"Uh-huh."

"I could've slipped, fallen, landed on my head, and died, but I did it anyway."

Dallin began to snore. It was a fake snore, intended to make Zoey think he was asleep so she'd stop talking.

"Hey, remember the time I made two hundred Sourdough Pistachio Carrot Cupcakes and I let you lick the beaters between each batch?"

"Uh-huh."

"That was cool of me, right? And remember the time I made you a two-gallon bucket of cookie dough for your birthday? That was cool too, right?"

Dallin ramped up his fake snoring, saying the word "asleep" on every exhale.

Zoey folded her arms on Dallin's bed, her elbows nudging his back. "It's hard to think of those things and not think I'm a good friend, you know? You're not the only one who gives and serves and sacrifices. I contribute. I give. Just because I'm busy doesn't mean I don't care."

Fidgeting, she sat upright, wagging a finger at Dallin as if he had eyes in the back of his head. "So if you're implying, Dal, that you're the better friend because you've worked at my restaurant every night and rescued us all from certain death, and I couldn't even make it to your one scrimmage, well, I take issue with that."

She paused, in case Dallin wanted to say something. He didn't.

"Still awake?"

"Sleeping."

Leaning back now, she perched the bottoms of her boots against the metal rail beneath the mattress. "It's not like the scrimmage was a once-in-a-lifetime opportunity. There's gonna be, what, like fifty more games this season?" Zoey paused. "Twenty-five, maybe?"

"Less talk. More sleep."

"Right. Yes. Go to sleep." Zoey closed her eyes, hoping for a nap herself. "Good talk. We're good. Everything's good. I have no reason to feel ashamed or guilty."

Dallin said, "You're still talking."

"I am? I am. I'm done. That's it." She straightened her legs, resting her ankles on Dallin's calves. "No more talking."

Silence. *Beep*. Silence.

Zoey laughed. "Hey, wanna hear something funny?"

"No."

"Remember when the brakes in Zoeylicious went kaput and we were zooming toward a cliff at a gazillion miles per hour? Well, I had one of those moments you hear about. You know, when a person's about to die and her life flashes before her eyes? It's not so much a visual flashing as it is a *feeling*, like a video on repeat, but it's inside your heart.

"You'd think my life-flashing or whatever-it's-called moment would be about cooking or critical acclaim or that serenity-now look people get when they bite into my hot, crispy Bacon Rings. But it wasn't anything like that."

The room was so quiet Zoey could hear the air whooshing out of a vent in the ceiling. She wondered if Dallin was asleep or still faking. Either way, she had to get this *loudness* out before it ate her alive.

"It felt like . . . how do I describe it? You know when you go to a restaurant, and you usually get the same thing every time but you think, 'Hey, I'll try something new'; then the whole time you're eating you're thinking, 'I should've got the thing I always get.' It was like that, only a zillion times bigger. I ached for a redo. I wished I could go back in time, blow off the *New York Times* people, and go to your scrimmage. Who cares if you didn't play? I wanted to be there."

Dallin was snoring. For real this time. Zoey wondered how much he had heard, how much he had missed. "I need some air." She got up and walked out of the room into the glare of a well-lit hallway.

Salt in the Wounds

 The Get Well Soon Diner was built in the 1950s and still looked like it: checkered floor, red booths and barstools, Elvis Presley and Chuck Berry posters, a cook in a soda jerk hat, a cashier in a poodle skirt and bobby socks, a jukebox in the corner. The jukebox was silent at the moment, thank goodness. Six a.m. was too early for rockabilly and doo-wop.

The diner had windows, even though it was *inside* the hospital. Zoey sat in a cold booth, peering out at the scenery: a gift shop, an elevator, a plastic ficus tree, a young man in scrubs on a cell phone, an EMERGENCY PERSONNEL ONLY sign on two closed doors.

The scrambled eggs were bland and the bacon was soggy, but the coffee was strong. Zoey was on her fifth cup, grateful for a caffeine reboot after an intense and sleepless night.

The booth faced an old TV fastened to the ceiling. The news was on. Closed-captioning made up for the low volume. Dread and angst filled Zoey's heart as she awaited coverage of last night's disaster.

She didn't have to wait long.

There was Zoeylicious, one end teetering over the edge of the cliff, the other end smoking like a chimney, ashes dancing in dawn's young light. A man's deep voice said, and captions read, "Carnage and mayhem last night as San Francisco's most talked-about restaurant, Zoeylicious, ravaged downtown in a high-speed blitzkrieg of terror and destruction. The restaurant's owner and chef, Zoey Sara Lee Kate . . ."

A photo flashed onto the screen. It was Zoey, dressed in a peach toque and jacket. Her mouth was open and her eyelids were in the middle of a blink, so she looked like a dazed drug addict. Zoey hadn't seen that photo before. She wondered who had taken it and how the news station had come to obtain it.

"Those closest to Zoey Kate describe her as a disturbed individual with a propensity for kicking puppies and voting Republican."

On-screen, animated horns sprouted from Zoey's head, and digital fire shot from her droopy eyes.

"Horns? Really?"

The screen changed (thank heavens) to a clip of Chef Cannoli in his kitchen, draping fettuccini noodles over a drying rack. The footage was old. Chef Cannoli's hair was thick and black, his stomach flat. His smile was as sweet and endearing as ever.

"Chef Zoey was one of three nominees competing for *Golden Gate Magazine*'s distinguished cooking award, the Golden Toque. Chef Pao, nominated for his seventh Golden Toque, forfeited the competition after he and most of his staff fell ill. Channel Five News has received confirmation that this year's winner is Chef Benedetto Cannoli of La Cucina di Cannoli."

"At least Pao didn't win," Zoey said.

Her phone beeped. A text from Gershwin:

How are you? How's Dallin? When you're ready to come home, call/text and I'll pick you up.

She wasn't ready yet. The hospital had become a sanctuary of sorts. To leave the sanctuary was to face real life. How many lawsuits awaited her? Would civic officials press charges? Would the reporters seek interviews to chronicle her despair? She couldn't face all that. Not yet.

She gulped down the last of her coffee and left the diner. She didn't know what to do with herself. Dallin would still be asleep, and Zoey didn't want to hang out with his mom. Walking felt good, so she wandered the hospital, up and down corridors and hallways, up flights of stairs, down elevators. The more lost she got, the better she felt. *If I don't know where I am, then no one else will find me.* It was as close to disappearing as she could get without a counterfeit passport and reconstructive surgery.

At length, in a hallway on the sixth or seventh floor (she wasn't sure which), she walked past the hostess from New Shanghai. The little woman sat on a chair, eyes glued to her BlackBerry. Her black hair was frizzy. He eyes were bloodshot. She didn't notice Zoey.

Two nurses walked out of the nearest room, leaving the door open a crack.

"Food poisoning, my eye," one nurse said. "He looks like he drank a tub of arsenic."

"Should we notify the police?" said the other nurse.

"It's the doctor's call," said the first nurse.

Passing the room, Zoey's nostrils twitched. *Seaweed. Tobacco.* She stopped. She looked around. The nurses turned a corner. The hostess was lost in BlackBerry land. Quick as a cat, Zoey slipped inside the dark room.

Chef Pao lay on his back in bed. His eyes were open. His lips were parted. His face was the color of stale mango peels.

"Looks like someone got a taste of his own medicine," Zoey said.

As soon as she said it, she regretted it. Seeing him in this condition—so sick, so feeble—made her heart ache. Chef Pao had been a thorn in her side ever since she'd made him a scallop dumpling. Still, she derived zero satisfaction from his suffering. Her business was excellence, not revenge.

A weak groan stumbled from Chef Pao's dehydrated lips. The fingers of his left hand twitched, beckoning Zoey to come closer. *Why?*

Curious, she walked to Chef Pao's bedside, saying, "I don't get it. For two decades, you've run one of the finest, most acclaimed restaurants in the world. You've passed countless health inspections. But yesterday, of all days, you and half of your staff get food poisoning. What happened? Did you get your eels from the dudes in bowler hats at Pier 39?"

Chef Pao reached for her hand. Since he was too weak to hurt or threaten her, she allowed him to clasp her fingers. His skin was hot. His grip was gentle. *"Láo . . . shǔ."* His breath smelled like dog puke on sauna coals.

"You want your shoes?"

No, that wasn't it.

"*Láo shŭ.*"

"Want me to call a nurse or . . . ?"

Chef Pao's eyes burned with desperation. At least, his good eye did. His bad eye had nothing going on. It just sat there, looking gross.

"*Láo* . . ." His frail hand raised Zoey's hand an inch. ". . . *shŭ.*" He moved her hand down and up again, mirroring the rise of the tonal vowel.

He wanted her to say it. Why?

"*Shoo-uh,*" she said, doing her best to imitate his vocal inflections. "*Lah-oh. Shoo-uh. Láo shŭ.* Is that right?"

Chef Pao nodded. Maybe. Might've been a long blink. "*Zài chúfáng.*"

"Can you say it in English?"

Chef Pao made a fatigued, *English-take-too-much-work* face.

"*Zài chúfáng.*"

"I got an app on my phone, it'll transl—"

"*Zài chúfáng.*"

Maybe this was a confession: a little "deathbed repentance" before meeting Saint Peter or Confucius or Buddha or whoever was waiting for him at the pearly gates.

"*Zài chúfáng,*" she repeated.

Chef Pao gave Zoey's fingers an encouraging squeeze. "*Kŏnghòlì.*"

Zoey said it back. "Kong . . . ho . . . ?"

"*Kŏng. Hò. Lì.*"

"Kong holy?"

"*Kŏng hò lì.*"

"*Kŏng hò lì?*"

Chef Pao released Zoey's fingers. He closed his eyes. His head sank into his pillow.

"What's it mean?" Zoey said.

Chef Pao was still.

Zoey walked out of the hospital room. She didn't know what to make of the encounter. All she could think was, *Láo shǔ zài chúfáng. Kǒng hò lì.*

Whatever that meant.

Yeah, About That

At eight-ish a.m., Zoey wandered back to room 304. The bathroom door was closed. She heard a running faucet and Dallin beatboxing while he washed his hands. Dallin's mom had arrived at five-ish a.m., but she was gone now. Stepped out for breakfast, probably.

Zoey plopped down onto the armchair next to the bed. At the foot of the bed sat a box of Kings County Jerky: Grass-Fed Original. Tied to the box was a ribbon attached to a shiny helium balloon with a football helmet on it.

While Dallin washed and beatboxed in the bathroom, Zoey took out her phone, put it on speaker, and said, "What does '*láo shǔ zài chúfáng*' mean?"

A woman's robot voice replied, "Book in kitchen."

Either Chef Pao was delirious or Zoey had pronounced it wrong. She tried again. "What does '*láo* . . .'" Up on the *a*. "'. . . *shǔ* . . .'" Down and up on the *u*. "'. . . *zài* . . .'" Down on the *a*. "'. . . *chúfáng* . . .'" Up on the *u*, up on the *a*. ". . . mean?"

The reply: "Rat in kitchen."

So New Shanghai had a rat problem? Rat germs could

certainly make an entire kitchen staff sick. Or was "rat in kitchen" a reference to a traitor in his midst? Someone close. Someone he trusted. A friend turned saboteur.

In either case, what did Zoey have to do with it? Why had Chef Pao made such an effort to tell *her* about it?

"What does '*kong ho li*' mean?"

The reply: "Empty hole E."

Meaningless.

She tried again. "What does '*kǒng hò lì*' mean?"

The reply: "Oh intimidation in."

"Thanks for nothing." She put her phone in her skirt pocket, attributing the meaningless message to sick delirium.

Dallin came out of the bathroom, wearing a hospital robe over his dirty clothes. He stopped beatboxing.

"How's your head?" Zoey said.

"Awesome," Dallin said, giving two thumbs up. "Coach came while you were gone. He brought me jerky and a balloon. Did you see?"

"Yep." They were the focal point of the room. How could she *not* have seen?

Dallin walked back to the bed, a spring in his step. "Coach heard about how I busted down the door last night in Trolley Three. He said I'm a hurricane. He's gonna start me at our next scrimmage, play me the whole game."

"Awesome. When is it?"

"Wednesday, seven p.m., at Everett."

"I'll be there."

"Promise?"

"Cross my heart and hope to eat meat loaf."

"Suh-weet."

"Unless I'm in prison," Zoey added. She still had a gazillion dollars of property damage to answer for, as well as possible criminal charges. The phrases "criminal negligence" and "attempted vehicular manslaughter" knocked around in her head.

Dallin sat down on the bed. He lifted the lid from the Kings County Jerky box. "Dude, Z, did you swipe my jerky?"

"No."

"Someone opened the bag and took some."

"Maybe it was your coach."

"It was closed when he left. I checked."

"Your mom?"

"She left before coach came."

"Maybe a nurse did it."

"Nurses don't steal jerky."

"Don't look at me. I don't even like jerky."

"Well, the jerky didn't steal itself."

WHAM.

Zoey bound to her feet. "Say that again."

"The . . . jerky didn't steal itself?"

Zoey closed her eyes and held her fingers to her temples. The events of the previous four weeks raced through her mind like a filmstrip on high speed. She observed every moment, every step, every glance, every word. She gathered a phrase here, a silhouette there. A stutter. A scowl. A rat skull. An empty shelf. An invitation. Chopsticks. A ponytail. A coincidence.

And then, like a key in a lock, everything clicked.

"Say '*kung ho li*' ten times fast."

"We're not talking about my jerky anymore, are we?"

Zoey clasped Dallin's face in her hands and planted a big kiss on the top of his head. "I'll see you at your scrimmage." She dashed out of the room.

Racing down the hallway, toward the elevators, she whipped out her phone and made a call. He answered on the fourth ring.

"Knuckles, where are you?"

"I'm, uh, let's see . . ." Static. Rustling. Wood legs sliding across a concrete floor. ". . . under a table, looks like."

"You're with the Night Owls, aren't you?"

"Uh, hold on." More rustling. "Monk? Four? Other ones?" More rustling. "They mussa took off after the brawl."

"You got in a fight?"

"Relax. We were on th' same team. Fat Jo's got a wicked left hook. It's the drummin', I reckon."

"I'm sorry I asked. Where are my trolleys?"

"At Hog Vomit."

"Meet me there in thirty minutes."

"I don't wanna m—"

"*Knuckles.*"

Rustling. Grunting. Boots on broken glass. "See you in thirty."

Investigating

 "In here," Zoey said, leading Knuckles into Trolley 3. Jagged pillars of dusty sunlight stabbed through the cracks and holes in the windows. Stepping over dried stains on the floor, Zoey couldn't tell if they'd come from spilled food, spilled drinks, or spilled blood.

Arriving at the emergency-brake room, she stooped down to inspect the door frame. Crusty gray goop, bumpy to the touch, caked the inner panels. "Is this . . . ?"

"Cement," Knuckles said. "Chef Pao musta snuck in here yesterday and sealed the door to the frame. Tha's why the door wouldn't budge."

"You're half-right," Zoey said, brushing flakes of dry cement off her fingers. "Wait a minute. You were in the trolleys yesterday. How did someone sneak on board without you knowing?"

Knuckles plunged his meaty hands into his jeans pockets and looked down at his big black boots. "I mighta, kinda sorta, stepped out fer a bit."

"You *what*?"

"I got hungry, walked down t' the Chevron station, bought a corn dog and Skittles."

"What kind of Skittles?"

"Wild Berry."

"I love that kind."

"They're tangy." Knuckles scratched his hairy chin. "I was gone twenty minutes. The meddler musta been watchin', waitin' fer the right moment."

"Fifty bucks says he tampered with the brakes and gears too."

Outside again, Knuckles lay down on his stomach and crawled under Trolley 1. "Don't bump yer head."

Zoey got down on her hands and knees and followed Knuckles under the trolley. The dirt was damp and ashy. The air stunk of burnt oil and rust-bitten metal.

Knuckles rolled onto his back. He pointed up at a white tube that ran the length of the undercarriage. "See this tube? It's the brake line. It's been slit open witta knife. Last night, we had enuff juice in the line t'make the brakes work fer a half hour or so. Once the juice drained out, the brakes went dead and we were in trouble."

He pointed above his head at an elaborate system of metal arms and hooks. "See these gears here? They connect to the levers in the driver's box." Propping himself up on one elbow, he reached up into the metal maze. "I feel sumthin'. It's lodged up in there real good."

Knuckles bit his lower lip as he tugged on whatever object was lodged inside the gear system. *Snap!* Knuckles withdrew a long black rod, the ends of which had broken off.

"This explains a lot," Knuckles said. "The meddler placed this rod in such a way that it wouldn't jam till I shifted tuh third gear. Tha's why the gears didn't jam at first. I hadn't gone above second."

Knuckles looked up. His eyes fixed on something. "Is that . . . ? Hold on a sec." He reached up into the gear system. He arched his back and rotated his arm. "Almost . . . got it . . ."

Clank! Ping!

Knuckles lowered his arm, clutching an object in his burly fist. He reached toward Zoey and uncurled his fingers. "Recognize this?"

In Knuckles's greasy palm lay a gold lion's head, four inches tall, its jaws open in a silent roar.

The Cupcake

La Cucina di Cannoli was a media circus. A gaggle of cameramen and reporters faced a square table at the center of the dining parlor. At this table sat Chef Cannoli, bright-eyed and clean-shaven, dressed in his finest kitchen whites. The other tables and chairs had been moved to the back of the parlor so nothing could stand or sit between Cannoli and his press.

Zoey stood by the front doors, next to the empty umbrella stand. Through a gap between two brunette reporters, both of whom needed more fat in their diets, Zoey could see Chef Cannoli, his hands clasped on the tabletop, a genial smile on his tan face. He appeared so pleasant and harmless that Zoey nearly forgot—and had to remind herself—what he really was:

A cheat. A betrayer. Unworthy of the title "Chef." He almost killed me. My family. My best friend. My customers. He destroyed my restaurant. He cremated my professional reputation. He caused zillions of dollars of damage to this beautiful city. And for what? His name on a trophy.

A reporter said, "Chef Cannoli, you've been nominated

for the Golden Toque many times, but never won. After all these years, how does it feel to finally come out on top?"

A dozen cameras and microphones tipped in Cannoli's direction.

Cannoli placed his hand on his heart. "I cook for to give the happiness to the people, not for to win the awards. The Golden Toque belongs to the people as much as it belongs to me."

The reporters responded with looks of admiration. Zoey fought the urge to vomit.

Another reporter said, "What was the secret to this year's victory?"

Zoey wanted to blurt out, "Malice and subterfuge!" but she held her tongue.

"I have an angel watching over of me." Cannoli blew a kiss heavenward. *"Questo è per te, la nonna."*

The reporter sighed in an *ahhh-how-cute* sort of way. (If you've ever been to a baby shower, you've heard it. A lot.)

Another reporter said, "Chef Cannoli, your critics say the only reason you won this year is because Chef Pao and Chef Zoey were disqualified. Your response?"

Hot fury flashed in Cannoli's dark eyes. The flash was so subtle, so quick, that Zoey wondered if anyone else had seen it. Probably not.

"I no can speak for other chefs. I cook hard. I win award. If other chefs get the disqualified, no is fault of mine."

Zoey clapped both hands over her mouth to keep from screaming.

The press conference ended. Reporters traded microphones for lattes and cell phones. Cameramen packed up cameras and rounded up cables. None of them appeared to be in a hurry to leave. Good thing too.

Cannoli remained at the table, looking chipper and bright-eyed, advertising his availability for a one-on-one interview, should any reporters want one.

Don't mind if I do, Zoey thought, slipping through the media throng like a snake through a pumpkin patch.

When Cannoli saw her, he froze.

"Congratulations. The best chef won." Her voice sounded hard and cold. She would have to dial up the cheer, a lot, or this would never work.

"*Bambina,* what pleasant surprise is this."

His voice was level, cautious. He was too guarded. Zoey had to loosen him up. She tried looking him in the eyes. She couldn't. It was like looking at Judas Iscariot.

Which gave her an idea.

Planting her fingertips on the table, she leaned forward, lowered her lips to Chef Cannoli's cheek, and gave him a brisk, Italian-style hello kiss.

Drawing back to her side of the table, she watched the apprehension evaporate from Cannoli's jaw, neck, and shoulders. The tactic had worked. He thought she didn't know.

Cannoli reached forward and took Zoey's hand. (*The nerve!*) "*Bambina,* when I learned of your accident I had so much the sadness for you. Are you okay?"

"We'll see." Zoey withdrew her hand. She reached into her purse, took out a white container about the size of a

ring box. She lifted the lid, revealing a mini-cupcake with fluffy red frosting and white sprinkles. The cupcake was the size of a golf ball or donut hole. Bite-size. As much frosting as cake.

"I made this for you." Zoey placed the open box on the table. "It's a congratulations gift."

Cannoli slid the box to the side of the table. "*Grazie*. I put this in the fridge for to eat tonight."

Zoey slid the box back to the center of the table. "I prefer you eat it now."

Cannoli's eyes narrowed.

Uh-oh. Too eager? Did I tip my hand?

"I prefer it to eat later."

"Just one bite."

"After lunch, perhaps."

"Eat it."

"No."

Zoey heard the front doors open and close. She turned, looked. Two reporters had exited. More were on their way.

Zoey had one card left to play. The compassion card. She could only hope that somewhere inside Cannoli, beneath the greed and pride and ruthlessness, existed a teaspoon of compassion.

"I lost everything last night," Zoey said. "I'm bankrupt and jail-bound, and I'll never cook professionally again. I need to know that someone in this city still appreciates my cooking. Please, one bite."

Cannoli's face softened. Zoey saw sorrow in his eyes. Real sorrow, like the gravity of what he'd done was at last

sinking in. "I suppose one bite won't give me the hurt."
Cannoli picked up the cupcake. . . .

Attaboy.

He unwrapped the pleated cup. . . .

Good.

He placed the cup inside the box. . . .

Keep going.

He opened his mouth. . . .

Almost there.

He raised the cupcake to his lips. . . .

Yes. Yes.

He put the cupcake in—

"Chef, phone call." Panzanella appeared at the table, pretty as ever, her waist-length black hair swaying like a curtain by an open window. "It's *Taste of Italy*. They want an interview."

"Ah!" Chef Cannoli set down the cupcake without taking a bite. He accepted the phone. *"Ciao?"*

Zoey clenched her hands in her lap, resisting urges to chew her nails or claw her seat. *I am* not *loving* Taste of Italy *right now.*

Cannoli leaned back in his chair and crossed his legs. *"Gli americani non possono cucinare,"* he said with a laugh.

The front doors opened and closed again: the sound of more newspeople leaving the restaurant. The window of opportunity was closing. Fast.

The time for subtlety had passed.

Zoey reached into her pocket, took out the gold lion's head from Cannoli's busted cane, and placed it on the center of the table. This got Cannoli's attention.

"Hang up," Zoey said.

Cannoli obeyed. "How did you . . . ?"

He reached for the statuette. Zoey snatched it away before he could.

"A trade," Zoey said. "I give you the statuette. You eat my cupcake."

Cannoli balked. "Is poison."

"I assure you it's not," Zoey said. "This ain't New Shanghai, and I ain't you."

Cannoli's eyes darted left, then right, then: "Give it to me the lion head."

"No."

"I have a gun."

"No, you don't."

"Is under the table, in my right hand, has the aim at you. Give it to me the lion head and no one gets the hurt."

"We gonna trade or not?"

Cannoli clapped his hands on the table and twiddled his thumbs. (Surprise. No gun.) He weighed his options, then, "Yes, we make the trade."

"You first," Zoey said.

Cannoli was leery. "How do I know you will give it to me the lion head if I eat this cupcake?"

"I can show the press now if you'd like."

Cannoli picked up the cupcake. He smelled it, dabbed the frosting with his tongue. It must've smelled and tasted fine, because he popped it into his mouth. He held out his hand.

"Not until you swallow," Zoey said.

Cannoli chewed, and chewed, and swallowed.

Let the showdown begin.

Zoey set the lion's head figurine on the table. She didn't need it anymore.

With quick hands, Cannoli swiped the statuette and hid it in his pants pocket. "Get out."

"I will soon enough."

Cannoli titled his head to one side, wincing. "Something is . . ." He rubbed his throat. ". . . *ferito* . . ." He rubbed his palm across his forehead, raking away a layer of sweat. "Panzanella?"

The pretty server appeared at his side. Cannoli handed her the phone, saying, "*Acqua con ghiaccio. Fretta.*"

"*Sì*, Chef." Panzanella dashed off to the kitchen.

Zoey said, "Ice water? That's your plan?"

Cannoli said, "Hot peppers, that is *your* plan?"

"Not exactly," Zoey said.

Panzanella emerged from the kitchen with a glass of ice water. Cannoli gulped it down. He waited.

Panzanella took back the glass. "*Bene . . . ?*"

Cannoli's nostrils flickered. "Still burning."

Zoey said, "Mind if I grab a chair from the back? This might take a while."

Cannoli coughed and wheezed like he'd swallowed a flaming porcupine. Panzanella hurried back to the kitchen in search of something colder than ice water. An Arctic spring, maybe.

"Forty years . . ." Cannoli pounded his fists on the table, a rope of saliva dangling from his puffy lower lip. ". . . I work like the slave . . . but Pao . . . and *you* . . . is my turn . . . is my turn for win . . ."

A cameraman unpacked his camera and hoisted it on his shoulder. A reporter with wavy red hair and glue-on eyelashes stepped in front of the lens and raised a microphone to her chin. "We're live in La Cucina di Cannoli, where Cannoli appears to be having a heart attack. Will he live? Will he die? Will someone other than myself come to his rescue? Stay tuned as Channel Three brings you this breaking story."

The other newspeople scrambled to unpack their gear, eager for their own pieces of the breaking news action.

Cannoli's face was redder than a garden beet. He clutched the sides of the table, arms trembling. "*Buffone!* No is the heart attack. Is the peppers."

"And not just any peppers." Zoey spun on her heel to face the cameramen, all of whom had their cameras on their shoulders, tapes rolling. She held her arms out wide like a ringmaster welcoming an audience to a circus. "They're Trinidad moruga scorpions, the hottest peppers in the world. Cannoli here just ate five. You'd be surprised how small they get in purée form."

Panzanella came to the table with a glass of ice milk. Cannoli gulped it. Milk spilled down the sides of his chin, onto his white jacket. (If you're gonna spill something on a white jacket, may as well be milk, right?)

Zoey continued her address to the reporters. "Cannoli here thinks if he drinks enough cold stuff the burning will go away. He's wrong. He could lick the frost off Santa's sleigh; it wouldn't help. Only one thing will stop the heat. I'll tell you all what it is, but first . . ." Zoey winked at Cannoli. ". . . let's take a stroll down memory lane, shall we?"

Panzanella took the glass of milky ice cubes and stepped

back, unsure of what to do next. "Maybe we should call an ambulance."

A few reporters nodded like that was a good idea, but no one did anything.

"Let's see here." Zoey paced back and forth, hands clasped behind her back, like a lawyer in a courtroom. "Mr. Cannoli, when I informed you of my plan to open a restaurant, you discouraged me. You said running a restaurant is all work and no cooking: taxes, audits, employees, injuries, lawsuits, Code Browns, et cetera, et cetera. When that didn't work, you came to my house—uninvited, mind you . . ."

A reporter gasped.

"You said you had no idea who the third Golden Toque candidate was. 'It's between two Indian chefs,' you said. 'Close your restaurant for a night,' you said. 'Come work for me. Here's a check for an unholy amount of money! Help an old man, please, for the love of all that is sacred!' You knew *Golden Gate Mag* had its eye on me, didn't you?"

Cannoli's lips formed an O. He sucked air like a high-powered vacuum cleaner. The fresh air, cold in comparison to the goings-on in his mouth, may have provided some relief, but it wouldn't be enough.

"Two days ago . . ." Zoey lengthened her lawyerly strides to make full use of the space between Cannoli and the press. ". . . someone snuck into my restaurant—that's trespassing, by the way—and contaminated my ingredients with cockroaches, centipedes, and tarantulas. You wouldn't know anything about that, would you?"

A reporter tapped a cameraman on the shoulder. "You're getting this, right?"

"Oh, I'm getting it," the cameraman said.

"But you didn't stop there!" Zoey said. "That same night, at three in the morning, you sent one of your goons to tamper again with my trolleys." Zoey shot an accusing glance at Panzanella. "Isn't that right, *Ponytail*?"

Panzanella shrieked. "He made me do it! He bribed me! And blackmailed me! I'm too pretty to go to jail!" Bawling, she fled to the kitchen.

Tears skidded down Cannoli's purple cheeks. He wrapped his fists around his ears. "My ears! I can't feel my ears!"

"Your eyeballs are next." Zoey gestured to the cameramen and reporters. "Tell the fine folks of this jury what you've done, and I'll tell you how to stop the burning."

Snarling like a gassy pig, Cannoli pointed a quavering finger at Zoey. *"Ragazza male, fuori dal mio ristorante!"*

Zoey winked at the cameras. "I don't know what Cannoli just said, but I bet it wasn't 'More peppers, please!'"

The reporters and cameramen sniggered.

Resuming her lawyerly back-and-forth strides, Zoey spoke in a loud, clear, and dramatic voice so the news crews' microphones would capture her every syllable: "Last night, someone tampered with my restaurant's brakes, causing a multi-block traffic accident that nearly killed dozens, maybe hundreds, of innocent people. Tell us, Cannoli (if that is your real name), why you did it. Reveal your dastardly shenanigans to the world."

Cannoli collapsed to his knees, clutching the sides of

his head like his brain wanted to burst out of his skull. "It burns!"

The cameramen moved closer. Not to help, but to get better shots.

Zoey got in front of Cannoli. She leaned forward, her hands on her thighs, her face close to his. "This ain't complicated, *bambino*. You confess. I make the burning stop. The truth will set you free."

Cannoli's sweaty face contorted like bread dough in a KitchenAid Pro. His chest heaved. "The Golden Toque is *mio*."

Zoey *tsk-tsk*ed. "So stubborn." She turned and made for the front doors. The newspeople stepped aside, clearing a lane for her.

"But . . ." Cannoli reached out with both hands. "You cannot to leave."

"I know a lost cause when I see one," Zoey said, each step taking her closer to the exit.

She was bluffing, of course. She would never leave him like this. He might die or explode or both. She wasn't like him. She wasn't willing to kill to win, even if she was in the right.

Come on, Cannoli. Fess up.

She shoved open the front doors. The sounds of the city—car motors, hydraulic brakes, horns, sirens, seagulls, the bellow of a distant steamboat—quadrupled in volume. Stopping in the doorway, she turned, glared at her rival. "Last chance, Cannoli. Once I leave, I'm never coming back."

"You . . ." Cannoli wheezed, his shoulders heaving. ". . . are young and new. People . . ." He coughed, then gagged on the cough. ". . . like things new. In forty years, no one wi—" Wheezing. ". . . no one will have the care about you." Gasping. "No one is to remember your name."

"Suit yourself," Zoey said. The final bluff. Once outside, she'd be out of moves.

She turned 180 degrees.

She raised her right foot.

Her sweaty toes wriggled inside her boots.

She waited for Cannoli to break. *Say something. Call me back in. Please.*

Not a peep.

She glanced back to make sure Cannoli hadn't died. He hadn't. He was on his knees still. Watching.

Zoey stepped outside.

The doors closed behind her.

Epic fail.

Now what? Jail, of course. But after that? What am I supposed to do with the rest of my life? On the verge of tears, she considered her options:

Join the circus.

Move to a trailer park and adopt cats.

Join Knuckles's biker gang.

Move to Tibet, join the monks.

Embrace mediocrity. Live in obscurity. Never dream, never strive, never create. Work at TGI Friday's for forty years. Retire. Become "that weird old lady" who does her laundry in the bathroom sinks at the public library. . . .

"*IOOOOOOOOO CONFESSOOOOOOOOOOOO!*"

The cry came from inside the restaurant.

Thank goodness.

Zoey dashed back into the restaurant. The old restaurateur was on his knees, sobbing like a baby, clothes drenched in sweat.

"Talk," Zoey said.

Cannoli hung his head. "*Io confesso*. Everything Zoey said is truth. The bugs, the brakes, all of it. I did the sabotage to Zoeylicious. And New Shanghai. It was me."

A reporter stepped in front of the cameras. "Breaking news: Chef Cannoli's shocking admission that he, not Chef Zoey, is responsible for last night's vehicular rampage . . ."

Justice.

Zoey reached into her skirt pocket and took out a silver packet of Kraft Mayo.

Peanut Butter Milk Shakes

Zoey sat on a chaise lounge on her back patio, watching the sun set in the fog. For the first time in months, she wasn't dressed in chef attire. She had on a black hoodie and black jeans. Bare feet. It felt good to wear normal clothes. Relaxing. Liberating. Part of her wanted to never wear a toque and chef jacket ever again. The other part of her— the honest part—knew it was only a matter of time. You can take the chef out of the kitchen, but you can't take the kitchen out of the chef.

Gershwin walked out of the house holding two golden-brown milk shakes in Mason jars, with bendy straws. He sat down on the chair next to Zoey, handing her one of the milk shakes. In silence, they sipped and pondered and watched the boats and ferries dock at Fisherman's Wharf and Pier 33. Seagulls squawked. Engines *vroom*ed. Somewhere on Jefferson Street, a blues band played T-Bone Walker's "Stormy Monday."

"Penny for your thoughts?" Gershwin said.

Zoey didn't feel like talking. Except she *did* feel like

talking; she just had so many thoughts and feelings knocking around in her head she didn't know where to start. Except she did know where to start. She felt like . . . like . . .

"I'm just so sick of everything."

"Who are you and what have you done with Zoey Kate?"

"Not the cooking. I love the cooking. And I love sharing my food with other people. But everything else." She licked a glob of milk shake off the rim off her jar. "Royston Basil Boarhead posted a ten-page article online, chronicling his harrowing escape from 'Reaperlicious: Chef Zoey's Trolleys of Death.' He didn't even mention Cannoli. He knows it wasn't my fault. He knows I was sabotaged. He posted the article anyway. Oh, and get this: he called my Chocolate-Covered Pork Chops 'underwhelming.' One minute I'm Mozart, and the next I'm underwhelming. Can you believe it?"

"I can."

"Why aren't you as mad as me?"

Gershwin sipped his milk shake, his brow creased like he was deep in thought, giving careful consideration to what he'd say next. "This Boarhead guy, you place a lot of value on his opinion of you. Why?"

"He's an acclaimed food journalist."

"An acclaimed chef too, no doubt."

"Well, no." Zoey felt like she was back in New Shanghai, explaining the Golden Toque to Dallin. "Most food critics aren't chefs."

Gershwin smirked. "It's a funny little world we live in it, isn't it? Our film critics aren't filmmakers. Our book critics aren't authors. Our music critics aren't musicians. Our food critics aren't chefs. And yet we all put so much stock in what they say about us."

Gershwin had a point. Had Thomas Keller or David Chang or April Bloomfield called her pork chops underwhelming, that would be one thing. But Royston Basil Boarhead? What had he ever done besides write about what other people had done? Also, his mustache was stupid.

Gershwin added, "No matter what you do in life, no matter how much beauty and good you bring to mankind, there will always be someone there to criticize you. But time is on the side of excellence. History remembers the great ones: Bach, Shakespeare, da Vinci, Franklin, Chapman, Ellington, Einstein, Disney; but no one remembers their critics. Why? Because their opinions don't matter, and things that don't matter don't last."

"I wish I had a trillion dollars," Zoey said. "I'd buy a ginormous airplane and fly around the world and cook for every single person on earth. I wouldn't even charge money. I just wanna see people enjoy my work, you know?"

Gershwin raised his jar in a toast. "To the artist's plight."

Zoey clanked her jar against his. "To the artist's plight."

She drank.

Such a delicious milk shake.

Bad Timing

Zoey bounded out of her house, rocking an oversize T-shirt with Dallin's face on the front and back. A megaphone and sparklers jutted out of her purse. She carried a box of homemade macarons shaped like footballs. Zoey was ready for some football.

As she traipsed down her driveway, she kept her head down because, one, her red leggings and glitter-gold Doc Martens boots looked like Peanut Butter Twix wrappers, and that was awesome, and two, she wanted to avoid eye contact with the three reporters waiting on the sidewalk.

The time was 6:45 p.m., fifteen minutes until kickoff. The reporters—two women (one blonde, one brunette) and one man (Tall, Dark & Handsome)—had been there since noon, waiting, watching, pining for an interview. Zoey didn't know what news outlets they were from or how they had obtained her address.

By law, they couldn't step foot on the Kates' property unless invited, but they could stand on the sidewalk (public property) for as long as they pleased. The reporters acted like they didn't notice Zoey. Until she reached the sidewalk—then they sprang.

The blonde reached Zoey first. She jostled a digital recorder in front of Zoey's face. "Chef Cannoli claims he's innocent, that you fabricated the charges against him. Your response?"

Zoey was in no mood for interviews, but how could she *not* respond to that one? "Cannoli is guilty. We all saw his confession."

"Cannoli insists his confession was coerced," the blonde pressed, "that he was under physical duress and afraid for his life. He called you a 'delusional, sociopathic liar.' Your comment?"

"It's good to hear his vocabulary improving. Excuse me." Zoey sidestepped the blonde. "I'm late for an appointment." (She thought "appointment" sounded more urgent than "my buddy's football scrimmage.")

As Zoey marched up the sidewalk, the brunette walked alongside her like an excited puppy keeping pace with its master. "Chef Pao says he was cheated out of this year's Golden Toque prize."

"I know the feeling," Zoey said.

"Last night on Twitter, Pao challenged you to a cook-off: winner gets the Golden Toque."

"So I heard."

"Do you accept his challenge?"

"No."

"What are you afraid of?"

"Listen, the only thing I care about is great cooking and delicious food. Anything else is noise."

"Chef Pao says—"

"If another Golden Toque means that much to Chef Pao, he can have it."

The brunette fell back as Tall, Dark & Handsome caught up with Zoey. "You're the talk of the town, Chef. Most of it ain't pretty. We're offering you the chance to set the record straight. Why won't you take it?"

"I promised my friend I'd go to his game."

"Oh. Who does he play for?"

"The Marina Middle School Penguins."

Tall, Dark & Handsome made a *you-gotta-be-kidding-me* face. (If you've ever asked your parents to let you skip school because you had "the zombie flu," you've seen it.)

"Hold on, now. Think about what you're saying. I write for the *LA Times*. Blondie back there, the *Seattle Times*. The brunette, the *San Francisco Chronicle*. Combined, we got two-million-plus readers. You'd pass that up for a small-potatoes, middle-school football game?"

Nearing Hyde Street, Zoey heard a cable car humming up the hill: her ride.

"I'll have to catch you another time," she said, "because I wouldn't miss tonight's game for the world."

The Hurricane

The lights were on, the bleachers were packed, the marching band was playing "Louie Louie," the cheerleaders were doing whatever it is they do, and Dallin was leading his team onto the field. Zoey lead the fans in a chant of "PEN-*GUINS!* PEN-*GUINS!*" as she distributed sparklers and specialty macarons among them.

Dallin played a great game. In the first quarter, he got two quarterback sacks. In the second quarter, he blocked a field goal attempt. In the third quarter, he tackled the other team's water boy. In the fourth quarter, he intercepted a pass and ran the ball for a touchdown.

The fans cheered for Dallin, but no one cheered louder than Zoey. (The megaphone, remember?)

When the game was over, Zoey whizzed onto the field. Weaving through a fray of helmets, shoulder pads, and unholy smells, she made her way to Dallin. His helmet was off, his face sweaty, his uniform smeared in grass and mud. Were they not such good friends, Zoey might've thought he looked rugged and handsome.

Dallin raised his hands for a high ten.

"I don't think so," Zoey said, flinging herself at her best friend, wrapping her skinny arms around his thick neck. "I've been a self-centered snot burger and I'm sorry I skipped your scrimmage. Will you ever forgive me?"

"You're choking me," Dallin said.

Zoey squeezed harder. "Please forgive me."

"I can't breathe."

"I'm not letting go until you forgive me."

Dallin patted Zoey's back. "Hey, you came tonight. That counts."

"So we're cool?"

"We're cool."

Zoey released Dallin, but only for a little bit because as they trotted off the field, side by side, she wrapped her arm around his arm.

"Are you gonna fix up the trolleys?"

Zoey brushed a clump of grass off Dallin's cheek. "Nope. I got bigger plans now."

"Bigger than three trolleys and a jazz band?"

"Way bigger."

"So what are they?"

"You'll have to wait for the sequel. But enough about restaurants. Let's talk about your game. Number seven on the other team, what was his problem?"

"I know, right? After every tackle he'd tug on my leg hair. So annoying."

"Everyone was psyched when you hammered him. Even his parents applauded."

Dallin beamed. "I got him pretty good, didn't I?"

"Like a hurricane."

"Hold on."

Dallin stopped and turned. Looking back at the stadium—the lights, the empty bleachers, the haggard players, the happy fans and families, the odors of dirt, grass, blood, and sweat—he smiled. He looked so content, so *football-is-awesome-and-as-long-as-I'm-here-I-have-nothing-to-complain-about.*

Zoey decided to apply the same attitude to her cooking. Forget the media. Forget the awards. Forget the attention. Slow down. Enjoy every taste. Every smell. Every texture. Every color. The looks on people's faces when they bit into something delicious.

They continued homeward.

Dallin said, "Hey, what should we do tonight?"

"I feel like cooking. How does pizza sound?"

"Suh-weet."

"What sounds better: Bacon Chestnut Mushroom or Thai Peanut Chicken?"

"Pepperoni."

"Pepperoni and what?"

"Just pepperoni."

"So . . . no twists, no ethnic blending, no innovative flair, just plain ol' pepperoni?"

"You can throw some cheese on it if you want."

"Huh. I've never made a just-pepperoni pizza. Sounds fun."

As they walked into the night, Zoey held Dallin's arm tight, cherishing how real it felt—the skin, the hair, the dirt, the scars, the bruises . . .

It was better than holding a trophy.

After-Dinner Mints

🥄🥢 After a four-week trial, a judge sentenced Chef Cannoli to fifteen years in prison. Cannoli spends his days volunteering in the cafeteria. His fellow inmates say the food has never tasted better.

🥄🥢 After seizing all of Chef Cannoli's assets, including his restaurant, Mulberry Bank declared Zoey's debt "paid in full and then some."

🥄🥢 Knuckles and Miss Lemon got married, then moved to Mexico to "lie low for a while." Once a week, Zoey gets a phone call from Knuckles's parole officer. "Hey, you haven't heard from Knuckles, have you?" Zoey plans to change her number.

🥄🥢 Unable to choose between two adoring women, Four tried dating them both: one on weekends, the other on weekdays. The scheme lasted forty-eight hours. He's single again.

🥄🥢 Dallin consumed fifteen Domino's pizzas in one hour, earning him a spot in the Guinness Book of World Records. Tums offered him a college scholarship.

Valentine bought a new trumpet. Monk bought a new piano. Bird spilled coffee on said piano. Monk took Bird to small claims court. A judge told Monk and Bird to get over it. Gershwin bought a new hat.

Fat Jo gave up donuts, got way into yoga, and lost seventy-five pounds. No one knows what to call him now.

Chef Pao is still a jerk, but his moo goo gai pan is tastier than ever.

Royston Basil Boarhead had a falling-out with his mustache. No one recognizes him anymore.

Jambalaya Barbos still lives in his parents' basement.

Under new management, the Rainy Days Diner was converted to a Chuck E. Cheese's. *SF Weekly* deemed it "the most depressing Chuck E. Cheese's ever."

Chef Zoey Kate divides her time between the Hurricane Dal Fan Club (she's the founder and president) and plotting her next restaurant venture.

Greetings, fellow chefs!

Zoey Kate here. (Yes, *the* Zoey Kate.) Hey, remember all those awesome dishes you just read about? Well, today is your lucky day, because I'm about to share three of them with you. I hope you're not wearing shoes, because I'm about to knock your socks off, Zoeylicious-style!

But first, disclaimers:

According to my lawyer, the agents at Allstate Insurance, and the doctors at Memorial Hospital's Burn Center, not all kids are genius chef prodigies. As such, I must advise you not to attempt any of these recipes without the assistance of a parent or legal guardian. That way, if you accidentally cut off one of your fingers or burn down your house, you can't sue me. (I *so* don't have time for a lawsuit right now.)

Also, taking into account that you probably don't have a fire pit, and that some cooking skills (instinct, gut feelings, oneness with ingredients) are unteachable, I've made minor alterations to my original recipes in hopes of maximizing your chances for culinary awesomeness.

Enough talk. Let's cook.

The World's Greatest Chocolate-Covered Pork Chops

Serves 1

Ingredients

1 bag Ghirardelli Dark 60%
   Cacao Squares, 80 count
4 Peanut Butter Twix bars
6-pack bottled water, distilled
24 ounces Eagle Ranch Pistachios
   (optional)
1 change of socks
1 sturdy backpack*
1 ride to the airport

1 plane ticket to San Francisco
   International Airport
1 map to 816 Francisco Street (if
   I'm not home, wait on porch)
50 bucks
1 tip
Altoids
Gas-X (recommended)

1. Board plane.
2. Enjoy flight with above-mentioned provisions.
3. Take cab to 816 Francisco Street.
4. Eat pork chops I serve you upon arrival.
5. Let food digest before walking.
6. Replace socks.

*I recognize that not everyone has access to a sturdy backpack. So, for my backpack-challenged readers, I've included a Plan B recipe on the following page.

(The World's-Not-Greatest-But-Still-Pretty-Darn-Tasty) Chocolate-Covered Pork Chops

Serves 2

Chocolate Mole Sauce
2 tbsps coconut oil
4 cloves garlic, minced
1 medium onion, chopped
2 medium tomatoes, chopped
1 tsp dried oregano
½ tsp ground coriander
1 tsp cumin
¼ tsp cinnamon
2 tbsps chili powder
4 cups chicken broth
2 tbsps raisins
3 tbsps slivered almonds
½ unripe banana
2 ½ ounces 86% dark chocolate, chopped

Apple-Cranberry Compote
2 Granny Smith apples
2 tbsps butter
¼ cup dried cranberries
2 tbsps brown sugar
¼ tsp cinnamon
⅓ cup cold water
2 tsps cornstarch

Pork Chops
2 six-ounce boneless pork chops
Salt, to taste
Pepper, to taste
1 tbsp butter
Freshly chopped cilantro, for garnish

1. First, make chocolate mole sauce. Melt coconut oil in a large saucepan over medium heat. Add garlic, onion, and tomatoes, and cook, stirring occasionally, until onions are translucent. Add oregano, coriander, cumin, cinnamon, and chili powder, and stir to combine.

2. Add chicken broth and increase heat to medium-high. Boil for 10 to 12 minutes, until liquid has reduced by about 25%. Remove from heat and let cool for a few minutes.

3. Pour mixture into the pitcher of a blender. Add raisins, almonds, and banana and blend on high until smooth.

4. Pour mixture back into saucepan and set over low heat. Add chocolate and stir thoroughly to combine. Cover and move saucepan to back burner over very low heat to keep warm.

5. Next, make apple-cranberry compote. Peel, core, and quarter apples. Cut into slices ¼-inch thick.

6. Melt butter in a skillet over medium heat. Add apples and cranberries and toss to coat with butter. Sauté, tossing occasionally, until apples are tender and just beginning to brown, about 7 minutes. Add brown sugar and cinnamon and toss to coat apples evenly.

7. In a small bowl, combine cold water and cornstarch. Whisk to combine. Add to skillet and cook about 30 seconds more, stirring as sauce comes together. Remove from heat, cover to keep warm, and set aside.

8. For the pork chops, season both sides of each chop with salt and pepper. Melt butter in a skillet over medium heat. Add pork chops and cook until golden brown on first side, about 4 minutes (longer if chops are thicker than ¾-inch). Flip and cook on second side until golden brown, about another 4 minutes. Center of chops should be opaque with no pink remaining.

9. To serve, divide apple cranberry compote between two plates. Place a pork chop on top of each compote portion. Spoon chocolate mole sauce generously over pork chops. Garnish with freshly chopped cilantro, if desired.

10. Remove socks before eating. Just to be safe.

S'meesecake

Makes 1 nine-inch cheesecake

Crust
1 ½ cups graham-cracker crumbs
(11 full sheets, crushed)
¼ cup sugar
5 tbsps butter, melted

Topping
1 ½ cups mini marshmallows
2 1.55-ounce milk chocolate bars,
coarsely chopped
Caramel sauce, optional

Filling
4 eight-ounce packages cream
cheese, at room temperature
4 eggs, at room temperature
1 ¼ cups sugar
1 cup sour cream, at room
temperature
1 tbsp vanilla

1. Preheat oven to 350°F. Grease the bottom and sides of a 9-inch springform pan.
2. In a medium bowl, combine graham-cracker crumbs, sugar, and butter, and mix well. Press crumb mixture evenly into bottom of pan and about 1 inch up the sides to form crust.
3. Bake in preheated oven until edges begin to brown, about 10 minutes. Let cool. Reduce oven temperature to 325°F.
4. Once crust has cooled, wrap bottom and sides of pan with a large sheet of aluminum foil. Then place wrapped springform pan inside a roasting pan. Set aside.
5. Fill a medium saucepan with water and set over high heat to boil.

6. Place cream cheese in the bowl of an electric mixer and beat on medium speed until creamy. Add eggs one at a time, mixing at medium-low speed just until each egg is incorporated, before adding the next. Scrape down sides of bowl with rubber spatula. Add sugar, then sour cream, and finally the vanilla, mixing after each addition. Be careful not to overmix, as this can cause the batter to form air bubbles.

7. Pour batter into the prepared springform pan. Smooth out the top of the batter with a rubber spatula. Pour boiling water into the roasting pan until it comes about halfway up the sides of the springform pan. Place in oven and bake for 1 hour. Turn the oven off. Do not open oven door or remove cake from oven for at least 2 hours. This is to prevent the cake from cracking.

8. Remove springform pan from water bath and discard aluminum foil. Cover and refrigerate overnight.

9. Prior to serving, preheat oven to broil. Run a thin knife around the inside of the springform pan and remove ring. Spread mini marshmallows in a single layer on top of cake, pressing in very gently.

10. Place under broiler just until marshmallows are golden brown, about 30 seconds. Sprinkle chopped chocolate over marshmallows and serve while marshmallows are still warm. If desired, drizzle each slice with caramel sauce.

Cucumber Lime Delight

Serves 1

Ingredients

1 lime	1 cucumber
1 tbsp honey	1 cup ice
1 tbsp club soda	Lime wedge, for garnish

1. Juice lime into a small bowl, yielding approximately 2 tablespoons juice. Add honey and club soda and whisk until combined.
2. Peel cucumber and cut in half lengthwise. Use a spoon to scoop seeds out of one half. Save second half for another use. Chop scooped-out cucumber half into a few pieces.
3. Pour lime-juice mixture into the pitcher of a blender. Add cucumber chunks and ice. Blend on high until smooth.
4. Pour into a wineglass and garnish with a lime wedge.

You're welcome.

—Z

MANY THANKS ...

...to the Father and the Son, for a million answered prayers.

...to Kate, for loving and encouraging and baking and being-proud-of-me-ing.

...to Zoey, for inspiring.

...to Dallin, for being.

...to my parents, for laughing at all the right parts.

...to Jun Wang, whom I met in a library, for the Chinese lessons.

...to my agent, Sara Sciuto of Fuse Literary, for her awesome.

...to my editor, Kieran Viola, for her also awesome.

...to Heather Crowley, editorial assistant, for her stellar editorial assistant-ing.

...to Jessie Ward, chef extraordinaire, for channeling Zoey to come up with the awesome recipes included in this book.

...to the 49ers water boys, for keeping our team hydrated.

...to you, for reading. (Also, you look great today. Have you lost weight?)

You're done.

Go eat some cookies or something.